THE JULIETTE SOCIETY, BOOK III:

# THE MISMADE GIRL

# THE JULIETTE SOCIETY, BOOK III:
# THE MISMADE GIRL

## SASHA GREY

**CLEiS**
PRESS

Published in the United States by Cleis Press, an imprint of Start Midnight, LLC, 101 Hudson Street, Thirty-Seventh Floor, Suite 3705, Jersey City, NJ 07302.

Printed in the United States.
Cover design: Scott Idleman/Blink
Cover photograph: iStock
Text design: Frank Wiedemann

First Edition.
10 9 8 7 6 5 4 3 2 1

Trade paper ISBN: 978-1-62778-182-4
E-book ISBN: 978-1-62778-183-1

Library of Congress Cataloging-in-Publication Data is available on file.

*To all of you.*

# PROLOGUE

KNOWLEDGE IS POWER.

At least that's what we're told. It's another of those pretty sayings that is meant to tempt us or condemn us, put the onus of our decisions back onto our shoulders, weighing us down with our agency like a yoke. If you don't bother informing yourself, whatever happens next is your own fault because you chose to be ignorant, right? It's what they want us to believe so we'll look inward when things go wrong instead of trying to burn the system to the ground.

But then they tell us ignorance is bliss and make that side of the fence look pretty damned appealing when we've seen too much, known too much, done too much, and long for an escape. And yet, we can never truly go back once we've crossed a line. Pandora's Box can't be closed once the lid's been cracked open for a harmless little voyeuristic peek. Things can't be unlearned. So, if we look, we must plow ahead, forever changed by the things we know—even if no one can see the information burning beneath our skin, inside our minds and hearts.

Knowledge *is* power. Application of that knowledge is wisdom, but it's also complication, for what are you going to do with the things you've learned? Offense, defense, weapon or shield, the things we learn can make us actively powerful or passively strong. It's all about the choices we make.

Three years ago, I left a towering monolith in the desert after finding out a lot about the world I live in...and myself. I lost myself inside the life of a dead woman, a provocateur named Inana Luna, whose life mission had been creating art through the medium of sexual imagery and acts meant to push the limits of what sexuality is.

I found The Juliette Society again.

I had a surreal threesome with DeVille and his double.

A USB stick had been placed in my possession with the invitation to go a little further on my journey of self-discovery—for that's what it was. The choice was mine to make.

Though I'd had no idea it was a path I was taking at the time, I chose to tell Inana's story instead of living more of mine. I chose to tell everyone about who she really was, who women like her, true provocateurs, really are—and why we need them in the world. Her story was more important in that moment to me than the journey deeper down the rabbit hole of The Juliette Society, though I left their name out of the story I gave to my newspaper for obvious reasons.

It was my choice not to look at the contents of the flash drive right away. It disappeared from my possession when I went back home and handed in my article, and I took that as a sign from TJS that our time together was over. I'd diverged from one destination when I'd chosen to go ahead with Inana's story instead of choosing to stay with TJS, and while I don't know what I'd have found, I lived with my decision. I've lived well with it. Profited.

At the time, it made sense.

The article led to interviews, the biggest of which being with my old buddy Forrester Sachs. Ironically, he probably knew Inana better than I did, having frequented the secret rooms beneath the hotel she worked at enough to be a VIP member himself. I saw him there strapped down while a dominatrix rammed a Jesus-on-the-cross-shaped dildo the size of my forearm in a very uncomfortable place.

Sitting with him, being filmed while he looked austere and serious in a three-piece suit, asking penetrating questions (pun intended), made me want to laugh. But the interview was important and it was perfectly executed, maybe because he'd known and cared about Inana too. Besides, he owed me a favor for my silence—not that I'd have exposed him. Sometimes people's low opinions of you, or fears, will encourage them to be very accommodating.

The interview led to huge success, but not necessarily in the field I wanted. I'm still a reporter, not making movies like I dreamed of doing, but I've achieved a certain level of success. The doors the article opened weren't the ones I'd hoped to walk through, and yet it's only been positive from a career perspective, a vertical trajectory laden with prestigious opportunities other people would die for. Still, sometimes I feel as though I'm living someone else's dream instead of pursuing my own, not exactly content in this niche, but not dissatisfied enough to truly break away.

Lately, I've been wondering about the role fate plays in our lives. Are we freed of the womb at our births only to be shackled by the invisible chains of destiny? Despite our best efforts, are we trapped on a wheel of predestination? Struggle or acceptance, will we end up exactly where we were meant to?

Because if everything is predetermined, what choices are we actually making? Is it the illusion of choice, the idea of free will that keeps us getting up every day, or is that not an option at all either but another thing beyond our control? Maybe fate is a construct designed to make us feel safe when things in our lives spiral out of our control. Fired, cheated on, a friend passing away. God meant this for us, life meant this for us, the universe needed this to happen so we'd learn a lesson and grow as a person. We never get more than we can handle. When bad things occur, it's easier to accept them if we have the comforting blanket of destiny to curl up with at night.

I remember how it all felt being there three years ago, embracing the side of myself who was always waiting in the shadows for me to step aside and let her play. These days, vanilla is the flavor of the day… Maybe a little swirl action, if you catch my drift.

After Jack and I split, after I chose saving a dead woman's reputation and legacy over decadence, nothing was the same. I wanted things from Jack that he wasn't capable of giving me. After years of being together he was no longer interested in the simple pleasures of discovering my sweet spots. The Juliette Society gave me that. Becoming Inana gave me that. I was tapped into my entire being in a way that I could only describe as seeing myself inside and out.

But by becoming Inana I also sacrificed those experiences when I chose to save her. In reality I had everything and nothing was left at the end of the day for me.

Casual hookups became awkward moments, sex was different. I can't say it was as unfulfilling as not being appreciated or having zero spontaneity with Jack—but it became a new self-discovery in finding sexuality again. I was able to feel and smell and get excited because of what my body now knew. What I knew. What made me tick, and what just didn't work. I felt stronger and more confident in me than I ever have.

Even if I had to sacrifice TJS, even if I had to discover there was a side to Jack that I never wanted to admit existed, I was and am whole.

But I can't quite forget what happened. The flavor of letting go. The feeling of what happens when you become sensation and lose yourself completely inside your body. Silk and satin are nice on the skin, but I wanted to wear the red of stinging flesh and the rippled edges of rope indentations.

To this day, they're the most beautiful things I've ever worn. I took them off and haven't felt the press of a rope in years. This is the version of myself I traded everything in for. Maybe I never really had a choice…

I still don't know if fate is real. Did I settle for having a successful career instead of chasing my dreams and breaking every limit of who I thought I was? Who I could be? Maybe. Would I be in a better place if I'd plugged in the USB and dived into the contents? What reflection would I find in the mirror if I'd gone down that path?

I'll never know.

Regardless, I've had three years to wonder if I made the right decision that night.

# ONE

THERE'S A LEVEL OF WEALTH most of us will never fathom. Oh, we've all fantasized about becoming wealthy. We've all dreamed of winning the lottery, or finding a rich relation we never knew about passing away and leaving us their obscenely large fortune. There were always the kids who you envied that had a maid, heated pool and Jacuzzi, a room dedicated to video games and movies, and whose parents always had the kitchen full.

The fantasies aren't uncommon. We want the dream. Children and adults. No one wants to struggle or spend the best parts of their life working themselves to death, waiting for life to begin after their retirement when they're too old to do the things they'd always wanted to try.

That's why the fantasies are appealing—they're all the riches with none of the work—instant wealth without having to build an empire yourself, for that takes too much time for us in this culture of instant gratification. Who's got the time to devote to that when they spend half their time trying to take pictures of their lives to convince others they're doing better than they are?

But there's a level of wealth that brings more than just security to those who attain it—it brings pure, unadulterated indulgence. Luxury items most of us would work months or years to save up to pay for and treasure—new designer shoes, a crocodile Birkin bag, a flashy car—become disposable to these people almost as a matter of show, simply because they can.

Imagine:

Your favorite musician playing at your birthday party. In your house.

Fleets of Ferraris.

Private jets on standby—even for fifteen minute long flights.

Penthouse apartments with the best views.

Celebrities at all your parties.

Blowing the yearly salary of the average American in an afternoon shopping spree.

Michelin star meals as a matter of habit rather than a once in a lifetime experience.

I've even seen a picture of a rose gold Hublot watch...on a dog.

See, these people have all of these things and more—and don't give a shit. But we're not talking about the one percent.

We're talking about the percentage of the wealthy inside those upper echelons who leave these millionaires behind. Their garages are bigger—and probably nicer—than your home. Their yachts hold submarines and helicopters.

Sheikhs and tycoons and dot commers. A good portion of them are economic meritocrats, having made their fortunes themselves, often at the expense of others. But some have been born into this tax bracket and wallow in it. They don't live in the same reality as the rest of us do. How can you when you're someone like Donald Trump's youngest son who it's said doesn't have his own room—he has his own floor in his parents' residence.

The children of these people will only "know" what hardship is like when they're raising their humanitarian profiles by volunteering in soup kitchens, or doing mission work in Africa or South America. Their stresses are different than ours, as are the doors that automatically open at the color of their credit cards or the whisper of their last name. The prestige their parents worked hard for is theirs automatically and they milk it hard enough to bruise the teat.

Which brings us to the Rich Kids Of Instagram. I'm pretty active on social media for work as well as the fact that now more than ever, our lives are happening online, but I'd never heard of RKOI until I looked up Jacob—my date for the evening.

You know that obnoxious friend you have who spends twelve minutes before each meal trying to snap the perfect picture for their Instagram? The one who doesn't enjoy any given experience because they're too busy snapping selfies to participate? RKOI are these people to the *n*th degree, only they're capturing the life of your dreams. Usually the children of barons, oligarchs, and moguls, they were born into this lifestyle and document it like they get royalties from the photos. It's like some of them have made Instagram their jobs, updating with pics designed to flaunt their wealth and privilege in your face.

Receipts to boutique designer shopping trips in the tens or hundreds of thousands, bottles of rare champagne being shaken and sprayed into the ocean from a yacht, casual snaps of them surrounded by friends in exotic locales—they're glimpses behind the curtain and they make sure it's even better than you imagine it to be.

Self-validation? Maybe. But wouldn't you like to try that lifestyle on and see how it fits?

My date is one of these Rich Kids.

He's got one of those trendy, big, white watches strapped to his wrist, but hasn't even glanced at it once in the hour we've been here at the restaurant. Other than on ludicrously rich men over fifty, I haven't seen a watch on a man in ages—don't get me started on Fitbits—and became curious as to whether it was decorative or functional. But he didn't even look at its face when I asked him what time it was to prompt him into it. Instead, he pulled out next year's smartphone and fiddled with that, hoping I'd notice, hoping I'd care about his toys.

There's a certain expression that crosses a man's face when he's trying to impress a woman. A suggestive half-squint while he's carefully sifting through his vocabulary to choose the right words as though he's staring into the sun to find them, only in this case the bright object is one he's acquired instead of the one at the center of our universe. They're one and the same to him in that moment, though, and he thinks the world should stop and marvel at the fancy object he's showing off.

I don't. What's the point? True wealth hides itself in quality whereas new wealth is insecure and flashy, begging to be noticed, seeking validation like that sexy thirty-year-old man whose ego is still bruised from being a nerd in high school and so he womanizes as hard as he can now to make himself feel better. A man who should understand what it's like to be overlooked, but becomes just another fuckboy. It's a treadmill of affirmation that never works because insecurity is an insatiable black hole that never gets fed enough.

Besides, I'm not wowed by possessions. The more I'm plunged into situations with the rich and famous, the more I find myself drawn to intellectual stimulation instead of pretty faces and flashiness. Last week I got caught up in a conversation with a complete stranger about predetermination and free will that got me into such a frenzy, I ended up screwing his brains out in his car as though I could take in the deliciousness of his intellect through osmosis and come.

I used to dream of dating a man who would sweep me off my feet. Then I wanted someone to sweep me off my bed with long thrusts. Someone who would ask, "What's new for you? What's something sexually you've been curious to try?" And I'd say, "Can we fuck while high and while eating churros? Or pizza? Can you text or call me the next day with lots of dirty sexy talk to tide me over till the next time we get to fuck? And if the next time we fuck isn't with each other, I need you to be okay with that. Can you massage my feet and tell me how badly you wish you could always be inside of me? Can you finger me discreetly under the restaurant table?"

And he'd say, "Done and done. When do we start?"

But they never do, and I can't imagine this guy's going to be any different.

My date must catch the disinterest on my face. "So, Inana Luna." He leans in closer. "Did you get to, like, see private videos she made? She seemed wild. How freaky did she get behind the scenes?"

I take a sip of the cloyingly sweet white wine he ordered for me to wash down the bitterness. I wanted everyone to remember Inana Luna's name, to remember her as more than the whore-like model the media painted her as when she died. I had no idea there would be people using her name to suck up and feed from my notoriety and try to use it to get an in with me, hoping that would turn to an in with someone higher up the social ladder than myself. Sometimes I wish I could make some people forget her name so I could protect us both.

I don't want my entire career to be defined by my article on her— no one wants to be pigeonholed. But at the end of the day, I can't change people's perception of me. I can only focus on putting new things out there and hoping people respond well to my efforts. Haters gonna hate, and vultures gonna swarm. It's the way of the world.

But this guy wants to talk about freaky? He's a novice. They all are. If I said, "I want your hot come dripping down my thighs and then I want you to lick it up and eat me out and make me come over and over again," he'd counter with, "Can I skip the lapping of my own jizz part?" And if I said, "No. I want you to love every bit of my delicious, sweet, wet pussy," he'd say, "My jizz ain't tasty."

Yet he'd still expect me to gobble it back like it's the newest taste sensation. I don't mind, but kink is about pleasing both partners.

I've noticed the average man is only kinky when it comes to coming on us. Tits, ass, face, they think that moment of power is the hottest. But you want them to truly get kinky, and that's when they get squeamish.

I set down my glass. "With her, what you saw was what you got. Part of the beauty of Inana was her lack of guise and guile. Her journey was one of transparency and she documented it well, trying to capture that. I did get to see inside her thoughts a little, though…" I trail off rather than mention the specifics of her diary, as a protectiveness surges through me. Her diary was about finding the limits of herself artistically through the medium of physicality and sexuality.

And part of me lost myself inside those pages. For a while, I was Inana Luna. I went to her house, slept in her bed wearing her clothes, drank coffee out of mugs her lips had once touched. I got myself off in her bathtub. I opened pages of the books on her bookshelves, and I discovered her secrets inside them, following the trail to Max Gold's hotel where Inana worked as VIP Concierge…and where she was Gold's lover.

I became his lover too, though that's part of the story that didn't make the final version when I released it to the paper. I wanted to be her. For a while I was, until I realized I had growth of my own to focus on.

Now, my date smiles at me, waiting while I formulate my responses. I don't know if he's truly interested in her or interested in trying to find a way to interest me, but talking about the specifics of her diary would be like tearing open the heart and soul of a ghost and ravaging the contents for another's amusement or small talk fodder.

I refuse to cheapen her legacy and my experience by doing that.

He prompts me when I don't continue. "You used to date a politician, right? Jack something?"

Jack. But he hasn't been my Jack since the night at Gold's hotel when he fucked me on the floor before leaving me for another woman. I saw him twice after that encounter, both times his eyes had lost their warmth when they looked at me. He'd been determined to turn me back into a stranger as though our relationship had never happened, erasing our intertwined lives as though they had never left a mark or mattered. Despite the fact that ultimately we weren't meant to be together, it hurt like hell. I mean, fine, break up with someone, but don't try to pretend they never existed.

Right after Jack, I dated a guy. I broke up with him with the standard, "it's not you, it's me" speeches when really I wanted to leave a note saying, *You had a kind of smallish dick but I kept on having sex with you because a) I wanted to know if I had a loose or tight pussy b) I wanted you to fall in love with me c) I hoped that your dick could get bigger.*

I mean, dicks are not beanstalks, but there's growers and showers. And—this happened once—some people take a while to get turned on to the biggest extent. Another guy I dated was one of them. It did get bigger.

Jacob, my date, leans in conspiratorially when I nod about dating Jack. "What's it like being that close to DeVille? Jack was one of his aides, right? And you were with Jack for years while going to school." He rattles off a few of the articles I've written and my stomach tightens as his questions become more and more pointed and personal.

A year ago, I decided to draw a line beneath the past and carry on with my life—difficult when certain events in my past are my bread and butter and I have to talk about them to promote myself.

"It feels like you've gone all quiet," Jacob says. "I'm not going to tell anyone what you say, if that's what you're worried about."

Well, I wasn't…until he just said that.

Jacob is clearly a fanboy of my work but hid it in our interactions until we met in person. This date has taken a turn, feeling more like a job interview. Most dates with new people seem like that; we must get to know each other with questions and answers, some sharper than others, but all of them with the purpose of getting to know the person. Yet Jacob here only seems interested in certain aspects of my life—namely, my career. Perhaps his disinterest in the rest when I attempted to engage him in other topics of conversation was feigned, designed to get me to prattle on more than I normally would in an attempt to prove myself somehow or to snag his interest. If you don't fill the silence, the other person probably will.

Is that what he was doing before turning the conversation toward Inana and my passions and my past?

Now, I'm not comfortable talking to him; his questions are so strangely personal I feel like he almost might be wearing a wire to do an exposé on me later. It wouldn't be the first time someone tried to turn my stories around and make me the subject of something salacious. When you're a young, attractive female in Hollywood, you become fair game for the sexualization of the talent machine to grind up and spit out. I'm not saying it's right—in fact, I think it's disgusting. But it's the reality of the industry whether you're an actress, or a woman behind the camera, and why I prefer print to television. If you're on camera long enough, people start to pay more attention to the way you look and how pouty your lips are instead of the words coming out of them. Look at any news anchor when she first started her career, then catch a glance at her five years later to witness her cosmetic journey. Watch as she grooms and styles herself into a different person on the transition to becoming a plastic version of themselves. Better hair, bigger tits, smaller waist. More makeup.

But it's funny how changing the little "imperfections" can make someone go from interesting to plastic and almost a less attractive version of themselves. Actresses ruin their careers doing this. Have you seen some porcelain veneers in bright sunlight? Cheek implants, lips overblown with collagen, faces paralyzed by Botox so you're never sure if the smiles are fake. To be fair, they probably are all fake, anyway. It's scary.

It's scarier how they're shamed into doing it by threat of irrelevance. There aren't roles for women over a certain age—we've all seen comedic sketches about that very thing. Our culture—and the Hollywood scene in particular, prizes youth and beauty above all else, and scoffs at anything less than perfect, calling those people unfortunate enough to have been born without flawless genes, "character actors."

It's not a testament to their acting abilities: it's a commentary on their appearances.

And I'm so tired of the need to be careful with the things I say.

"Let's talk about you for a bit." I smile to take the edge off my words.

He sets his phone back on the table. "What about me?" He takes a sip from the fancy blue cocktail he ordered, not caring that it looks like it should be the featured cocktail at a Mexican resort—or whorehouse. He's a rich kid and not my type, but he's fun in ways I've never experienced. I want this to be a good night. I need a good distraction.

I googled the shit out of him before meeting him tonight. Don't even judge me—we all do it. Social media lurking is the new black. His dad is a famous actor who married a socialite. Jacob doesn't really have a career that I've been able to find, and they don't usually call guys socialites, but that's basically what he is, dabbling in charity events and the music industry for a while. Mostly, he's seen at clubs and parties, and is one of the Rich Kids Of Instagram. If I'd known about that ahead of time, I'm not sure I'd have come on the date, which isn't fair of me to pre-judge, but there it is. We're all hypocrites in our own ways.

Jacob and I met in traffic on La Cienega. He was in the baby blue Lambo ahead of me at a red light, and I noticed him checking me out in the rear view mirror, revving his engine to get my attention. As though there's anything subtle about a Lamborghini in the wrong color. When I stopped behind him at the third red light in a row, he actually got out of his car and came back to talk to me as though we were in a club or coffee shop, not caring that he was holding up traffic—oblivious to the honking and shouting when the light turned green. The way he leaned against my car, casually flirting without a care in the world was embarrassing and kind of funny, and won me over enough to give him my number.

Jack was so serious and because of politics was always aware of people's perception. Jacob doesn't give a fuck about what people think—he only cares about having a good time. It's refreshing, if his application is somewhat immature. His displays don't come from a place of confidence—they come from insecurity, ironically because of his parents' success, but the veneer of self-assurance is thick.

Most kids are ashamed when their parents aren't successful. Not here in Los Angeles. Here they only care that their parents *appear* successful. Welcome to Hollywood, where status is everything, zip codes are God, and what the paint looks like is more important than what's under the hood. See, when you have auto-validation because of Mommy and Daddy, you get all of the privileged entitlement with zero accomplishments needed.

Celebrity kids don't need to do anything, they've already got a long leg up by simply being born to their revered parents. Not all celeb kids rely on their parents' notoriety, but a lot do. Even the good things Jacob does are funded by the trust fund given to him by his parents—and their connections provide the opportunities to set things up. Sure, people like him work, but most don't work for what they've got and don't care to learn what that's like. They're the worst.

I smile. "What generally fills your free time?"

He shrugs. "I don't know. Charities and stuff. Whatever."

Scintillating.

He turns to his phone again when it starts buzzing against the table, and I sigh, thoroughly disappointed. Dating's become less and less interesting. It's not that I'm looking to be in a committed relationship again right now, but I'd at least like my dates to be stimulating instead of feeling like a waste of my time. Where'd his intensity go? Some guys are all about the chase, but this is bipolar. He's either uncomfortably personal or completely disinterested.

But maybe it's because the juiciest details are ones no one else knows and I've never shared. Somehow I've become as careful as the politicians I hated Jack emulating.

Jacob finally looks up. "My friend's having a party right now. Want to go check it out?"

At least there will be fresh people to talk to. "Sure."

# TWO

⌒⟋⟋⟋⟋⟍⟍

WE PULL UP TO A HOUSE in the hills after a short drive—
then again, with the way Jacob speeds around in the Lambo, I'm
fairly certain he turns every journey into a short drive.

It's an older-style house, not like some of the newer modern ones
with razor sharp lines and metal and glass. Twelve or thirteen high-
end luxury cars litter the driveway, parked at strange angles, some
blocking others in for the duration, so I'm glad we're one of the later
to show up.

A burly security guard at the door actually asks to see our IDs
like it's a club, and we flash them. They must have had trouble with
underage drinking, or else this guy's been told to keep an eye out for
serious A-listers and to notify the host when they make an appearance—the more likely of the two scenarios. He asks the loud group of
friends behind us to stop laughing, as if it were a crime. I glance back
at them and shrug, just as confused as they are. You'd be surprised the
problems that can be paid to disappear when money is truly no object.

When we walk inside and there's no furniture in sight, I know the
party is going to be fucking weird. A guy with giant pupils and no

pants walks by with a towel around his neck, headed for the corner of the great room where a group of people look similarly messed up on something—probably mushrooms based on the way two girls sit looking at their hands and laughing. There are about nine of them sprawled out on the floor, tripping, talking about some really weird things.

"Let's go find something to drink. Maybe in the kitchen." Jacob leads me farther into the house. Still no furniture. It's either someone's place and they're moving out—or in—or it's a rental someone bought to be a party house, and doesn't care to deal with cleanup or repair costs or party casualties. Fair enough. I learned right off the bat never to host parties—the cleanup always ends up falling on you—and it's your things that get broken when someone's had one too many to drink.

Near an open glass door that leads outside to an enclosed yard, a group of guys in suits stand with plastic cups in their hands, taking turns furiously talking at each other, though no one's hearing anything based on the amount of coke they're loaded up on. Jaws clenched, faces sweating, periodic sniffing back the post nasal drip, I never saw the appeal or anything glamorous about cocaine. No one high on coke looks like they're actually having a good time—rather, it resembles someone just before they have a panic attack. They never stand around mentioning how good they feel; all you hear them talk about is finding more coke. At least the people on hallucinogens were discussing the nature of the universe and reality.

If I did drugs, I know which trip I'd rather experience. For now, I'll stick with tequila.

The kitchen's basically empty when we get there and when I see the selection, I get why. There's only drugstore-brand plastic bottled alcohol, no mixers, and no ice. No glasses either, only red plastic cups like a frat house party.

I guess this party caters more to the drug partakers—and alcoholics, judging by the lack of mixers—than those casually drinking.

Jacob pours four fingers of vodka into my plastic cup and gives an apologetic shrug. "Sorry."

I take a sip to show I'm game, but the sharp, cheap liquid burns like lighter fluid all the way down my throat and makes my eyes water.

Jacob nods at someone across the room. "I'll be right back, Catherine." He takes off and I take another sip.

Nope, I can't do it. I poke around in the fridge for anything to dilute the liquor in my cup, adding some ice from the dispenser, a little water, and a liberal douse of the lemon juice I find. Strange for a wealthy host not to actually care about their guests when it comes to drinks and food. Appearance and image is everything for this group of people and the lack of aesthetics and presentation for their guests is truly confusing. It's funny to think that growing up in my lower class neighborhood, families took pride in putting everything they could into a party. I get it though, fake bohemians who want to show they can get down and be authentic like the rest of us plebeians. But the facade doesn't work on me; I can see right through it, but I've been around it enough now where the sting is a little easier to take each time.

Blue-collar people seem to have more real fun, like they care about having a good time, not *looking* like they're having a good time. It's a small but important distinction. Non-celebrity partiers aren't at a party to be seen. They're there to cut loose after a long week, see their friends and maybe make some new ones. In Hollywood, no one has friends. They have contacts, acquaintances if they're lucky, but I wouldn't count on making any new ones here. Tinseltown is full of phonies and flakes—I learned that early on when arranging meetings with people. Trying to nail down interviews was a constant whack-a-mole game with people's schedules and appointments.

Drink marginally improved, I turn back to people-watch until my date returns. More guests have shown up and the music's gotten louder. Now that I'm not preoccupied with which drugs people are doing, I recognize a few people. There's a hot photographer here and a million young girls, barely twenty-one years old, clambering up the staircase to the house, their acts as cheap as their outfits, as they try to impress this guy. Like flies to a dead carcass, they cling to him, hoping to dip their fingers into his sickly sweet rot and feed off the prestige of being near to him.

Even better if they get to be the one sucking him off at the end of the night.

He doesn't care about them at all. It's so obvious. Everyone calls him "babe" or "sweetie"—I think because they don't actually know who he is but he's got a flock of followers so they think they should join in too. Strange they don't know who he is but they're right there too, in hopes to be his next side piece, or muse. I can tell it will never happen.

I've studied body language extensively in the past couple years to better read people when interviewing them. It helps to know how to get them to open up, to know when to back off instead of pushing harder and questioning them more aggressively. This guy only cares about one person: himself. The rest are as disposable as the red plastic cups we are all drinking from.

A hand snakes across my lower back and I turn to tell the person hands off, but it's Jacob. "Hey."

I relax a little. "Hey. I found a way to make my drink better."

He sniffs. "Oh?"

Oh. Jaw clenching, eyes brighter. If I had to wager a guess, I'd say my date leveled up on coke during his absence. Nothing flatters a girl more than her date needing to do hard drugs while in her presence. I'm not saying I'm as electrifying as blow, but it really grosses me out that he's done this.

He grins, oblivious to my regret at coming here with him. "Shall we walk around? Mingle? I'd love to show you off."

More like he'd love to move because his heart is racing and he's got the attention span of a gnat. Show me off? I swallow my pride and with a hint of grace, I am able to muster up, "Sure."

The mushroom party group has progressed to the stage where someone's dragged a lamp over to them, and they all stare at the jeweled facets as though they contain the meaning of life which will be unlocked if they look long enough.

A group of people bump and grind in the far corner—some more than dancing, if you catch my drift.

Jacob bumps fists with a few people as we make a circuit around the main floor, but doesn't introduce me to anyone or "show me off" which is a sweet relief. Most people are so obliterated at this point they wouldn't remember me unless I stripped naked and let people paint me with condiments they found in the fridge. Actually, that wouldn't work. There were no condiments in the fridge. Besides, with the string bikinis with postage-stamp tops that barely cover areolas, nudity wouldn't be memorable here.

I clock a forty-something guy with a goatee and sunglasses as a girl pathetically tries to flirt with him by trying them on, giving him her best *O* face. Jacob gives him a brotherly embrace and introduces me, the name sounding familiar. I hear a French accent so I kiss him on the cheek instead of shaking his hand. Jacob whispers something in my ear about him having just won best music video at some awards show, and I realize the goatee and I have several friends—acquaintances—in common, so it's more than likely he knows me as well. Now that I realize who he is, I feel slightly sick that I gave him a proper French introduction even though I shouldn't. People flock to him, telling him which project they just acted in, hoping to be the next star. Some don't care about being the star; they just want to get close enough to rub up against one for as long as it takes to shoot the video—maybe getting to fuck that musician in the video.

Groupies or wannabes. This party's met its quota for both.

A lithe blonde tosses her hair and rubs her fake boobs against the director's arm oh-so-casually. "People said my portrayal of hemorrhoids was so believable it made them uncomfortable to watch."

I bet it did. Sometimes I think desperation impairs one's thinking.

A curvy brunette steps forward and shakes his hand, though the gesture is surprisingly formal for people who have already been talking for a few minutes. "I was prominently featured in a commercial for IBS. It got national coverage."

While that would pay the bills like any other job, I'm not seeing how that would translate to the sexy vibe most music videos try to cultivate. They sell sex and sex appeal, and yeah, people catch things if they're not careful. STDs are becoming more and more common, but if you're the face of a genital herpes medication, that's a raging conflict of interest.

I turn to remark upon it to Jacob, but he's gone again. Probably to do another line in the bathroom. The body heat I felt beside me and thought was my date is actually a woman facing away from me, listening to a man talk about his new Maybach. Humble bragging is the worst. Either be proud of your possessions and accomplishment or be an insufferable braggart. Pretending to not be showing off wastes everyone's time when we all know you just want compliments and praise and attention. I'm sure he doesn't even have a driver and doesn't even know that the only purpose of that car is to have a proper chauffeur.

Sometimes I get the urge to find a group of people and say really random shit just to see who pays attention. Maybe something along the lines of, "I like to bite my toenails with my teeth. Sometimes my cat likes to eat the clippings." Sadly, in this town, people would probably think it was a new diet craze and say they've already done it. More likely it would be their personal trainer, or their cousin or friend who was the "expert." Everyone knows someone who's done the exact thing you're talking about, regardless of how inane our outlandish it is. Maybe it's the way they try to relate to other people.

It gets old fast.

I wander to another room and lean against the wall near two people obviously itching to get out of here to fuck, but getting through the preliminary "getting to know you" flirting. I say flirting, but they're pretty personal already.

She runs her fingers through her hair. "I also miss not worrying about STDs and being completely fulfilled, turned on, and proud whenever he'd come to completion and blow his load all over me and inside of me. We should have broken up before the first date, though."

The guy nods enthusiastically. "Yeah, nothing is hotter than making my girl come. I enjoy it just as much as my own pleasure. There's no self-esteem boost better than making a woman come all over my face or cock, especially when her moans get louder and faster and her muscles start spazzing. So hot."

"How do you keep going and not blow your load while she's coming on your dick?"

He shrugs. "Marijuana. Thinking about 9/11 now and then. Usually can last an hour."

Her eyes widen. "That's too long. Forty-five minutes is good. Twenty is fine, too."

He backpedals. "Agreed. But I can do it if need be! I can pretty much come whenever during sex. Mostly psychological."

Wow, and they say romance is dead.

She leans in, swaying a little. "I want to know if boning you on the actual 9/11 anniversary means you're extra hard for extra long."

He winks. "You could wait a couple months and find out for yourself."

*Never forget.*

I can't believe my date brought—and left—me here. He probably won't even notice the fact that I've left since he cares about one thing only tonight. Screw this, I'm out. Even if he rallied and came back more charming than ever, I'm not eager for the taste of his postnasal drip on my tongue from his goodnight kiss. I root around in my purse to grab my phone and order a rideshare when a stranger leaning against the wall by the front door catches my eye.

His dark blond curls give him an almost cherubic air, but the look in his eyes cancels it out, confidence bordering arrogance, and a smirk that makes promises my body decides it wants him to keep. I'd say he's a few years older than me, but something about his demeanor screams experience.

He's a man in a house filled with dudes, and it's very appealing.

I sip from my cup, painfully aware how hard it is to seem cool and sophisticated while drinking from red plastic.

He prowls over to me, directly, confidently, saying with his body "I noticed you, you noticed me, let's not play coy." He holds out his hand and I take it, noting the firm grip. "I'm Dominick. Nice to meet you."

"Catherine," I reply.

"Your date must be an idiot, leaving you all alone in a place like this."

I smile, not wanting to insult my date, but charity only goes so far. "I think he's in the bathroom."

Dominick inclines his head, getting it. "Then he's even dumber to waste your time while he does that shit. Your boyfriend?"

I shake my head.

He grins. "Want to get out of here?"

I contemplate leaving my date without even saying goodbye. In *Seconds*, a John Frankenheimer movie, there's a really great line I like that someone says to Rock Hudson after he awakes with his new face, having been given a second chance in life: "You are alone in the world, absolved of all responsibility, except your own interest."

That's exactly how I feel right now. For a while, I've been alone in the world, drifting aimlessly. We're all ultimately alone, despite the connections we make along the way to other people. And while the statement seems like it's giving permission for a free-for-all, it's really not encouraging you to hurt others. See, if we're at our happiest—psychopaths aside—we're good people. Doing things for ourselves that make us our highest form, our very best, only makes the world a better place. Sort of like Transcendental Meditation in a way, I suppose, but we can justify any choice with self-serving reasons if we try hard enough.

Would Jacob truly be sad if I went home with Dominick? Maybe. But I doubt it, and the way he was treating me wasn't respectful, what with the lack of care about me tonight, bringing me to a boring party like this and then disappearing. Anything could have happened.

Well.

I follow Dominick outside.

Something is going to happen when Dominick drops me off at home. I'll make sure of that.

# THREE

HE PULLS MY HAIR OUT of the way and kisses the back of my neck before I can get my key into the lock of my apartment door.

Turned on before I can turn the key.

His hands are on me before I can react, caressing the dip in my waist, the outside of my thigh, my shoulder. With the care of someone who knows a woman's body is made up of erogenous zones that don't involve the main five (breasts, vagina, ass, inner thighs, neck), he uses his fingers to slowly ignite the fuses of my body.

I'm wet before he spins me around and presses hard against me, kissing me slowly and deeply. Like he's savoring the way I taste, his tongue tangles with mine, plunging deep inside my mouth which makes me think of his cock plunging deep inside other places.

Hard door at my back, hard man at my front. I'm soaking wet, ripe for the plucking like fruit, waiting, swollen with juices.

I want him to squeeze me and make me drip all over him.

He reaches beside my ear and then I'm tumbling through the door he's opened, falling backwards but he catches me in his arms and kicks the door closed behind us with a loud bang. It's so protective and male it makes me want to swoon and squeal and give the neighbors another loud bang to complain about.

Dominick's hands roam all over, conquering instead of waiting for an invitation. Tentative lovers annoy me. Sometimes I just want to be taken by someone who knows exactly what the fuck they're doing without me having to draw them a map and explain a woman's anatomy.

He presses me against the wall and slides a hand up my shirt, undoing my bra and jerking it away like it offends him that it touches my skin. His hand is rough on my breast, and I gasp into his mouth when he squeezes it, pinching at the nipple. He rocks his hips against mine, letting me feel the hard length between us.

"What do you need?"

"I need to get fucked so hard. I haven't been properly fucked with a dick I loved and couldn't get enough of since my ex-boyfriend's, one year and four partners ago."

He grins. "What did you like about it?"

His hands on my body are driving me wild. "It had a slight upward curve that would reach my G-spot and was the first and only that could make me orgasm vaginally while fucking. It was a little too long for sex and hurt often for a long time. But then I got used to it and I even handled him fucking me with an inhumanly huge dildo in the later years, when we were bored of each other and didn't want to face the reality that we were incompatible and not really in love. And of course he could stay hard for a long time and I knew that I'd have a reliable ride."

He nips the skin of my neck between his teeth and I yelp, so turned on.

"I'll give you a ride you'll never forget," he growls.

I grab his ass and pull him closer, locking him against me so I can grind that cock where it's making me ache, but I want to feel his skin too, so I tear at his black button-down, frantic with hunger for his body heat.

He's muscular but lean, with a tattoo swirling across his ribs and up his chest, down his left arm, but I can't see what it is exactly because he pulls my shirt over my head and leaves it partway on, a makeshift blindfold and restraint. He's got my hands pinned above my head.

"Where does Catherine want it?" His breath is warm against my lips and I lean forward to kiss him, but he avoids it, wanting an answer.

"Right here…pinned against the wall."

He chuckles and I wish I could see the look in his eyes because the huskiness in his voice makes my wetness drip down my thighs.

"No. I meant where do you want my cock, but I like your answer very much. I'm going to remove my hands. You will keep yours against the fucking wall. Yes?"

I nod, a smile stretching my lips. It's been forever since someone bossed me around like this. My nipples tingle in anticipation for what he's going to do next. Part of me wants to know, but I'd rather not spoil the surprise, so I keep my hands up, glad to hear the tearing of a condom wrapper. Pleasure second, safety first.

He strips me from the waist down and I shiver, waiting for the blanket of pleasure he's going to put on me.

"Last chance to give me your input before I start."

I bite my lip. "Do I need a safeword?"

His teeth graze my neck. "Do you?"

Sometimes you just know a person, even when you've just met. I know Dominick likes sex the same way I do and that he'd never hurt me unless I wanted him to. So I shake my head. "You know what to do, don't you?"

His fingers deftly probe my drenched pussy and my breath catches at that movement. Right there. That one he does with a hooked finger that makes me want to follow him around while he makes come-hither motions inside me until my legs give out or we get to Alaska. "Yes, Catherine. I do know what to do."

I want him to fuck me now, pound as hard as he can inside me, but he removes his hand and spins me around, ass bare and out, posture the same as if he was frisking me.

Is that where the saying "getting frisky" comes from?

He spreads my ass cheeks apart and starts lapping at my asshole with his tongue, the unfamiliar sensation warm and dirty and so fucking hot I spread wider to give him more access.

I'll look up the etymology later.

His tongue swirls around and around and he pulls back, but replaces his mouth with a finger. "Has anyone ever eaten your asshole before?"

"If they had, it was a lick or two, nothing like this."

"Do you want me to fuck your ass?" He sucks a little at the skin again, and my knees weaken ever so slightly.

"Does anyone ever say no to you?"

"Not for a very long time. Most people like what I can do to them."

I lick my lips. "Then do whatever you want, Dominick." It's a bold invitation, but I know he'd stop the instant I told him to.

My lips are sealed.

He grasps my hips and tugs me out a little farther from the wall and then his cock is pushing inside me, but not in my ass like I was expecting. He's inserting himself into my pussy and he's got a large lollipop-cock, judging by the feel of the head going in. The shaft is girthy but the head is a little extra big, making it a tight fit.

That first thrust is always the best, especially when it's been a while. Especially when it's with someone worthwhile. He goes slow and deep, all the way in until he's nudging my cervix where he holds steady, giving me a minute to stretch and get used to his size. One hand reaches around to gently massage my clit, the other trails up to knead one of my breasts. I push back against him and then he starts fucking me in earnest.

With every thrust, his balls smack against my clit with a wet, meaty sound and it feels like someone lightly slapping it. I like it.

He slides one hand down the back of my neck and gathers my hair as he slowly pulls out of me, pushes back in, settling between my legs like he's in for the duration. I'm not sure what it is, strawberry maybe, but as the friction between us grows, the condom smells rubbery and sweet as though it's fruit that's ripening with my juices. He fists the hand that's holding my hair, sending a small, sharp tug of pain through my scalp.

I'm desperate for more, wishing for something to suck on because the primal way he's fucking me is too much and not enough and it turns me into a perfect beast in kind, made with the sole purpose of mindless fucking except I'm hyper-aware of everything going on and giving it my all with everything I've got. I want this to be as good for him as it is for me right now, and I circle my hips, making a nice, tight infinity pattern with them that pulls at his cock, making it rub new places inside me. He sucks in air through his front teeth. Perfect.

I can feel my orgasm building up inside like a goddamn symphony. Dominick shifts his weight and I'm going to come so hard I almost want to move so it doesn't feel quite so good so I can draw it out, slower, savor it longer, but it's like holding back a tsunami.

I lick my upper lip, tasting the saltiness of sweat and the remnants of my lipstick.

So good.

I shudder, my hips buck, and my limbs shake with the release and the sheer size of him inside me. My walls clamp down on him as he continues thrusting in and out of me, drawing more of my come out, spreading it around, making skin slide against skin. No lube feels as good as this. No lube comes close to feeling the way a woman's true attraction for her partner can coat them both, making sex so good for both of them.

Maybe a man's come, thick spurts of wet heat. The thought shatters me in the best ways as his hot breath puffs against my neck and I suddenly need to suck his cock.

I need to thank him for getting me out of that lame party.

I push him away and spin around, dropping to my knees and looking him in the eyes as I take his cock in my hands. His gaze sort of sharpens with interest when I peel off the condom and toss it away, guiding his cock towards my mouth. I slide my hand around between my legs before running it up and down the shaft of his penis a few times, coating him, making his cock slick with my juices.

He smiles and his pupils grow to the size of dinner plates, but he patiently waits.

I line him up but put his head near my cheek and I lick up the seam of his balls, leaving a trail of saliva. More natural lube. He nudges my lips with the tip of his cock and I softly swirl my tongue around the little hole, covering my lips with spit and he pushes a little deeper, advancing along my tongue as I flick it back and forth beneath the shaft, giving a suck to increase friction with a vacuum.

He splays his hands above my head on the wall, bracing himself so he can relax and enjoy the things I'm doing to him with my mouth. I let his cock come out of my mouth with a little pop and I lick his balls, one and then the other. He groans when I gently suck them both into my mouth, cradling them more than working them, letting him feel the heat of my tongue seeping into his skin. Balls are so damn delicate. Some men get squirrelly about partners touching them.

Not Dominick.

I swirl my tongue around them, then work my way from the base of his cock to the tip, up and up and up like I can't get enough of his soft-serve cone. I want him to melt on my tongue like it's summer, and I lick all around the big head and suck him deep again.

He shoves his cock so deep I can barely breathe, and I gag but keep going. I'm getting wetter, but I already had my turn.

I take what he gives, gripping his hips when he holds my head steady and fucks my mouth with shallow, frantic movements. I want him to come on my face, something I've never really wanted before or seen the appeal of, but I want his hot load in my mouth, to swallow it and have part of him inside me after he's left my apartment because there's no way in hell I'm letting him spend the night.

He bursts inside me, coating the surface of my tongue with a hot, salty tang, almost nutty and sweet, his body freezing as though all movement has been switched off except for his twitching cock.

He doesn't even breathe.

I let him slip from my lips when he inhales again.

We're on my balcony, Dominick having a smoke before he leaves, me keeping him company when he turns to me. "Tell me something personal about yourself."

Because I don't really expect to see him again, I tell the truth. "Recently I've wondered how different life would be if I were more attractive and better-looking."

He shakes his head. "Everyone wonders that. Angelina fucking Jolie wonders that. Everyone's insecure about their looks. Tell me something else. Something you fucked up."

People usually ask you to share something when they've got something specific in mind they already want to tell you about. Do they ask what you do? It's because they want to tell you what they do for a living, thinking it will be impressive. If someone asks about your hobbies, it's usually because they have one that they're itching to talk about. I decide to keep this about sex. "The last guy I fucked. Before you."

He squints. "What happened?"

"I messed up. It was because I drank five whiskeys. I fucked the wrong brother. I miscalculated when I picked the less attractive and more annoying one just because he was from out of town and guaranteed to go away after finishing our business. I didn't even come." What I don't tell him, is that night is basically when I lost interest in sex for quite a bit.

Dominick inhales and exhales a long cloud of smoke. "You're not shy talking about sex."

I shake my head. "I think that my next lover might be a woman; I've never been as close to the fantasy as I am now. I started looking online secretly and I just got my first flirty message from a female whose photos I'm not sure if I'm even attracted to." My pussy hasn't been this wet and throbbing in a long time. I don't know if it was from thoughts of the woman or from talking to Dominick about her, but there you have it.

"Is it because you can't find the dick you want? Or because suddenly you find yourself attracted to women?"

I shrug. "I've been with women before. Sex—good sex—isn't about parts, it's about experiences."

He mulls this over while I ask, "What did you really want to confess to me?"

"I knew who you were, through an acquaintance, when I saw you tonight at the party."

I'm surprised his confession isn't phallic. "You did?"

He nods and blows a smoke ring.

I take a sip of my water, mulling over his sudden confession before asking, "Were you told to fuck me?"

He shakes his head. "No, but I couldn't resist once I saw you."

"Who's the acquaintance?" I ask. I'd be mad, but this doesn't surprise me. L.A. is all about seven degrees of separation and using any in you can get. Besides, I just came really hard and am having trouble scrimping up the annoyance society thinks I should probably feel for Dominick.

"He's a wealthy European philanthropist who often donates to civil rights campaigns, and under the radar helps journalists get access and funds their trips to get across hot zone borders. One rumor is that he helped Edward Snowden safely to Russia with the help of other influential world leaders. Nobody knows for sure. But he requested to get in touch with you and that's why I'm here."

Maybe if I wasn't me, and hadn't experienced the things I've experienced in my life, this would weird me out, but it's not the first time I've caught the attention of someone with a political lead. You get photographed with a senator a few times and people start to notice. So, while not as direct as I'd like, it's still not completely unforgivably underhanded. As it is, it's the most interesting thing that's happened to me in months, maybe a couple years. "Why does he want to get in touch with me?"

"Have you heard of Benny Arthur?"

"Who hasn't?" Benny Arthur is a man everyone's salivating over, trying to get an interview with. He's come into the limelight in his own right after having run an investment firm with Senator Duncan—someone who was rumored to be the next POTUS until words like "Ponzi scheme" and "investment fraud" got bandied about. It's worse because he's based his whole image on being Joe American, honest as the day is long.

Somehow, he's managed to avoid truly being hurt by the scandal, but there are those who wonder what worse things he's done.

One skeleton in the closet usually means there are three buried in the backyard.

No charges have been laid so far against Duncan, but Benny would know if Duncan knew about the dealings or if he was a partner on paper only, as he claims.

A sanctimonious potential president who is comfortable ripping off old ladies of their life savings? Yeah, that's news.

Dominick crosses his arms. "Mr. X can get you an exclusive with Benny Arthur."

My stomach tightens just a little. If I got it—and the information was good enough to launch a tight story—this could be huge. But anything this good comes with a price, and I'm not naive enough to think it's going to be free. "He's legitimate?"

Dominic nods. "He is."

I can't say no. I need something like this right now. "Then you can give the man my contact info. Why wouldn't he just email me at the paper like everyone else does? My work contact information is online."

A smirk pulls his lips into a thin line. "He's very…particular about the way he operates. He likes to do things his own way." He pulls out his wallet and pulls out a card. Cream-colored with a simple but elegant spiral shape embossed on the sides. The only writing says "Mr. X" with a phone number beneath it. I take it, turning it over in my hands, strangely reminded of *American Psycho*. The choices put into business cards in that movie were obsessive and hilarious how they fixated on the tiniest detail from the font to the barely discernable fifty shades of off-white everyone had chosen as representations of themselves.

The room seems to shrink down to the size of this card, the air thickening and drying until it's like breathing through pages of an old manuscript and I'm slammed with a sense of being here before.

"What's wrong?" Dominick's voice pierces through the haze, and I blink hard and focus on his face.

"I just feel like this has happened before."

"Déjà vu?"

I nod.

He sits back and lights a cigarette. "One time at a party, someone told me that déjà vu is literal. You've literally seen that moment before, but not in this lifetime. That we choose everything about our lives before we live them, and that when we incarnate, sometimes we're so close to the life we map out that it gives us that weird sense of recognition."

I shiver. "Do you believe that?"

He laughs. "Nah, it was just some asshole on acid at a party. It was the most interesting version of reality I've heard, though. What do you think?"

I jab the corner of the card beneath my nail, grounding myself in the moment with that tiny bit of pain. "That the older I get, the less I'm sure of anything."

"Perfect reason to be a journalist is because you want to find out the answers to the world we're in."

# FOUR

✺

THE HARDEST PART OF SUCCESS isn't achieving it. It's trying to replicate it. You can't be content to simply get to the top—you've got to stay there as well. It's about staying relevant or else you'll become a has-been or worse: a one-hit wonder. Maybe it's safer to quit once you've made one great thing and coast on that greatness forever, sucking the teat of your former glory that no one can take away from you, but most of us have more to say from an artistic viewpoint than that one statement.

Besides, you never know if the sequel will hit harder, faster, better than the first. *The Godfather Part II, The Bride of Frankenstein, La Notte* (though I'd argue that *L'Eclisse* was superior and the best of the trilogy). Hell, even *The Empire Strikes Back* and *Terminator II* were better than the first installments.

Once you've hit it big, seen the other side of the fence, climbed that hill to the top, the follow-up is extremely important. Cripplingly important, really, as no one was expecting your initial success, so this time there's more external pressure sucking at you from the bated breaths of the audience waiting for your next move. "What are you going to do?" is a much easier question to answer than "what are you going to do next?"

I've found a little slack from the chains of expectation by being enigmatic in my answers. Keeping them guessing builds hype and garners more anticipation without me having to follow up or commit to any particulars. Now that I've seen success, I can't just work on anything; I've got to make a statement. I need to prove to the naysayers and myself that my success wasn't a fluke.

Part of me feels as though I lucked out finding Inana Luna. She was the perfect subject. Replicating that will be impossible, yet everyone thinks I'm cooking up something huge.

As of now, I've got nothing.

Oh, a few scandalous pieces here and there have kept my name in bylines and kept my juices flowing, but there's nothing that touches Inana Luna. Nothing that's grabbed me and refused to let go until I've sucked every secret from its lips. Believe me, I've tried to recapture it.

I click through my inbox one email at a time, not skipping a single one without at least skimming the contents for something, anything inspiring, but that's a relative term. Something that I'm invested in and something the wider public will care about is the intersection I'm trying to find.

People send their pieces or tidbits about themselves, hoping to make the paper, hoping to find a sliver of fame. I no longer reply to everyone, finding it too hard to come up with a nice way to tell them that the world at large doesn't care about their awesome niece who just graduated and is just the sweetest thing, or their dog who can "talk." I get a lot of letters from actors and writers, reaching out, eager to get some free publicity. I wish I could help everyone.

But I'm not interested in hollow stories. Feel-good pieces that only stick with you if you know the person the article is about, and fade away after a day or so if you don't—unless it goes viral. But even then, who hasn't had something go viral at this point? We as consumers are insatiable when it comes to entertainment, wanting more and more and more.

Baby goats, babies with evil eyebrows drawn on, everyone and their neighbor dancing to whatever trendy song everyone's going to forget about next week when another takes its place.

Entertainment for entertainment's sake is a great thing, but I need to make something different, something with longevity.

After the article came out, the offers started coming in. A trickle first, then a rush as word spread and nominations for awards hit my inbox. I had my choice of papers and magazines trying to headhunt me and entice me from the newspaper I was at. There was even an offer from a television program, but one short, lecherous interview later, I was completely turned off by that "opportunity."

I decided to take the offer Diane Fallows presented me with, mostly because of the magazine's impressive track record, but also largely because of the woman herself. First black female editor-in-chief by the time she was twenty-eight, she's intense in a way you'll only encounter in a handful of people in your life. She's got a quiet confidence lacking ruthlessness, and it reminded me of Inana. I wanted to see Diane in action, so I accepted her offer.

Three years later, I still haven't been disappointed by her, though I'm beginning to worry I'm disappointing her by not wowing everyone with another massive article. My Inana article was nominated for a Society of Professional Journalists award. I didn't win, but I didn't expect to even be nominated. Some thought my story was more provocative and edgy and should have taken the prize. Maybe, but it's subjective and awards aren't my thing. I wasn't going for a Pulitzer, anyways. I just wanted to tell Inana's story.

Diane does seem content to parade me around at industry parties, showing me off as though that's my contribution—bringing notoriety to the magazine.

I rub my knuckles against my lip, brushing skin against skin until my lip is slightly numb and tingly. This Mr. X interview could be the thing I'm looking for, despite the fact that I've wanted to stay away from politics for obvious reasons.

The hard part isn't finding a story everyone wants to hear about—hell, every tabloid rag and Buzzfeed list does that every day. I'm more selective because I have to care about the article too. I only want to work on stories that interest me and make me care. Maybe it's a sort of oppositional defiance borne of not being the filmmaker I wish I was right now, I don't know, but I think the magic ingredient is care.

Maybe I'll never find another story that overtakes me.

Maybe I'd be having this problem if I were making films.

Malaise. Life's been okay for a couple years now, but the glow's been slowly, steadily fading. It could be that I'm the one who's fading.

Is it better to succeed at a job you don't care about, or to fail at your dreams having risked it all? Either way you're not where you expect or hope to be. Maybe the discontent is in the wondering. They do say we regret things we don't go for.

But in this economy, it's good to have a job like mine that actually allows me to live comfortably. It's hard to give that up.

I scroll through the invitations in my inbox again. If I continue being successful as a person I'm not—for I am not meant to be this forever, surely—does that mean I'm actually right where I'm meant to be? Would that mean my dreams were never my fate at all, but a delusion or distraction?

For now, I'll stay here at the magazine, telling someone else's stories until I find the ones I need to tell.

Right now, the best lead is the one from Mr. X. As loath as I am to embrace the political world again, this is my career we're talking about. Some things are worth pressing pause on your aversions to them.

I pick up the phone and punch in his number.

# FIVE

I GOT IT.

Benny sang like the proverbial canary, not just implicating his old friend the senator, but burying him after a little coaxing on my part—not that he needed it. I got the distinct impression he was waiting to spill, but we had to build some suspense first.

We talked for a bit before I started recording—in this day and age, if you don't have audio or video, you're just asking for a source to pretend they didn't say something and then it's just your word against theirs, so I always play it safe. He mentioned Mr. X who, surprisingly, wasn't even there. I wasn't excited exactly to meet the man, but was very intrigued at the man who was able to get the interview of the year for me.

I was under the distinct impression of being under the micro-scope the whole time, though. Maybe it's just because of the unconventional situation, but it seems absurd and egotistical to me that someone would give me something like that out of the blue and then not show up to see how it went, or to even let me shake their hand in thanks.

The gentle sweetness of fresh roses fills my senses before I see the arrangement sitting in front of the door to my apartment. Two dozen red roses, artfully positioned in a square-cut vase.

Penelope.

I smile and do a slow spin, hoping to catch her peeking around the corner of the hallway, though that type of frivolity isn't quite her nature.

Roses aren't my favorite flower. They seem like the old standby when for the price, you can get much more original blooms that are underrated and equally beautiful. But roses are classic—just like Penelope, and from her, they always make me smile.

I pick up the vase, elegant just like her, and take it into my apartment, setting it and my purse on the counter so I can read the card. The small, printed words read, "Happy Birthday, Catherine. P."

I hold the card beneath my nose, practically smelling her Chanel No. 5 perfume on the card, even though there's no way she wrote on it or even touched it. I didn't realize how much I missed her until now.

I lean against the counter for a moment, my hip pressing the edge, letting the past overtake me with memories of France.

Penelope took me under her wing a few years ago just after Jack and I broke up. Not soon enough to head off the self-destructive spiral I began, tearing up online dating sites seeking external validation, receiving only disappointment. I'm lucky that's all I received with how reckless I was for that month, putting myself at risk, barely self-aware.

I was in mourning. I'd lost a long-term relationship, but I'd also lost Inana. Getting to know her by being her and then emerging from that cocoon of awakening was awful. It tore down who I thought I was, being Inana, and losing Jack.

Then again, I'd lost Jack before La Notte took over my life, heating things up in the desert. The Juliette Society saw to Jack and my separation, I'm sure of it. They set up the perfect distraction for

Jack in the form of a beautiful, fragile woman who needed rescuing. The victim-slash-princess to Jack's wannabe white knight. I guess I wasn't enough of a damsel in distress to appeal to the alpha male side of Jack that so desperately needed its ego stroked. I'd thought he was secure enough without that. A lot of incorrect assumptions were blown apart around then, shattered into pieces too small for wishful thinking even to put them back together. So, I was angry about that as well.

You hear people say they'd rather have the truth, no matter how painful it is. I'm one who shares that opinion. Yet it's hard to remember why that's your preference when you're standing in the rubble of the life you'd thought was truly perfect. For a brief, dark period after La Notte but before the interview caught fire, I dreamed of bringing them all down, not caring if the facts and lives I destroyed as collateral damage in the process piled on top of me until I was crushed by them—metaphorically and literally. If I couldn't have Inana, if I couldn't continue to be her, then why should the rest of them continue to be who they wanted in a place that wanted my silence as the price? I'd made my choice but wanted them to join me.

Perhaps that's why they gave me Penelope: to mitigate the potential for destruction I walked around with.

She contacted me with a plane ticket and an invitation to Paris the week the article came out. I'd have refused it on the grounds of it being strange and unsafe—in the age of the internet where everyone can hide behind a screen, it's universally unwise to get on a plane to meet a stranger for a coffee across the world. But somehow the fact that she was a woman made it feel safe and exciting.

Then the article came out and Inana's face and name were everywhere again, and it was a stark reminder of all I'd lost by rebuilding this woman's life and reputation at the cost of my own journey, even though she was already dead. And while the phone calls didn't get insane until a few weeks later with people wanting to interview me and talk about my work, I needed an escape.

Penelope was there with her classical beauty aesthetics, soothing me with refinery and a complete change of class level, never mind culture and scenery. She was a friend when I needed one. A shoulder; a mentor. Helen Mirren-like, I found her experience and age comforting. I trusted her advice and presence as you only can trust a stranger who has no expectations of familiarity with the way you are in the ways a friend does.

Not that I had many friends at that point. So much of my life revolved around Jack for so long to the point of becoming almost insular, now that that aspect was over, I was drowning in freedom on top of it all.

I needed Penelope. She was there.

She was—and is, as far as I know—a high-ranking Juliette Society member. I know they were handling me, using her to see how I'd react to the events of the recent past. But she told me the truth and asked me if I'd be able to "man up and deal" or if I'd let myself become a footnote in the history books of people who could have mattered if they hadn't self-destructed instead.

I loved her plain way of speaking, finding her directness refreshing after all the secrecy and political doublespeak I'd grown accustomed to while dating Jack and being immersed in that world where perception is everything and words are weighted to pull you down to your demise. You don't realize how exhausting those kinds of careful conversations are until you no longer have to deal with them, or be polite to people you think are horrible human beings.

So maybe they were right and I was a threat back then. I simply wouldn't have cared who I took down with me; I was simply sick of insincerity and lies.

Besides, when you're at your darkest hour, the best place to be is inside the City of Light. My heart—I'd been rubbed raw as though the first layer of my skin had been buffed by a slightly too exuberant exfoliation session or a sore hole after a dry ass-fucking. I was okay, but everything hurt and experiences stuck to my nerves, irritating and painful. My emotions were abraded and I needed soothing.

Drowsing around Paris slightly drunk on wine with Penelope was exactly what I needed. Thirty years my senior, she'd gleaned wisdom from things I'd never experienced and knew exactly the things to say to prevent me from further spiraling.

Even now, she remembered my birthday and took the time to send these beautiful flowers to let me know someone cares. I lean closer and breathe in the scent of the flowers before kicking off my heels and heading into the bedroom to change.

My room is not how I left it.

A flat white box lies across the foot of the bed, contrasting against my sage-green chenille throw blanket. Inside is a dress.

The fabric slips through my fingers like water, the satin so cool and soft it almost feels wet to the touch. The inky purple will make my eyes seem darker and reflect the shade of the dress, changing until they're more like a young Elizabeth Taylor's.

There's a note beneath the dress.

*A limo is waiting for you outside to take you to dinner. Happy Birthday.*

I scurry to the window and see the stretch limo parked by the curb.

Looks like I'd better hurry.

I walk back into my apartment after, a little baffled but it's amazing what a little lobster and a lot of melted garlic butter will do for a girl's mood even when she's eating an incredibly fancy dinner by herself on her birthday.

Penelope didn't show up and really, I should have known she'd be too busy to do anything but spoil me from afar. I kick my heels off and remove my hair from its chignon, wincing a little as my scalp protests the change. I gently rub the kinks as I head to the bedroom to change out of the dress.

I'm in the bathroom, having just washed the makeup from my face when my phone buzzes with the text.

Mr. X: *You looked beautiful in the dress. It's safe, then, to assume you like it?*

My heart speeds up after one dramatic thud that makes my lips tingle. I'd assumed the dress was from Penelope because of the flowers. If Mr. X was the one who sent the dress and paid for my meal that means he was, or had someone, inside to place the box on my bed.

How the hell did Mr. X get inside my apartment?

And what else has he done while here? I jump to my feet and pace around the bedroom, looking half-heartedly for wires or cameras, but stop after a moment. Men like Mr. X aren't the type to do anything stupid like that. They get off on power—like he did by giving me the interview with Benny, and then the dress, knowing that he could make me feel exactly like this just by mentioning the dress.

It's not just about the dress and my apartment being invaded. It's the fact he was watching me tonight—or at least that's what he wants me to think he did. Regardless of what he wants, I got a story. And he didn't actually do anything to me except give me a fancy dinner and a killer interview.

I reply: *It's beautiful. Thank you. I thought you'd be there today at the interview.*

Mr. X: *I couldn't make it. But congratulations and good work.*

Me: *Why didn't you come along for the celebratory dinner?*

Mr. X: *I had other things to attend to. But we'll speak again, I'm sure.*

I try to imagine him saying that with warmth instead of expectation.

# SIX

THE INTERVIEW HIT DURING AN otherwise slow news week…and basically went viral overnight a week later when Duncan was taken into custody and people get voracious for the scandalous details. I'm more than ready for them.

Diane invites me as her plus-one to an industry party to celebrate my interview's success. It's been getting huge airtime on television, especially with the senator's arrest. Benny's information was enough to put his old friend Duncan away for a long time—unless he buys his way out of it—and he gave it to the police just before he gave it to me. He didn't violate any laws with what he gave me, wanting to ensure Duncan got put away.

You never know. Sometimes the justice system doesn't work at all how it should.

No one thought OJ would get off, either.

Regardless, the interview solidifies my reputation for being tough but fair, and someone who will get the story no matter what odds are stacked up against me. It's flattering, but feels a little false, seeing as though Mr. X was the one who gave me the interview in the first place. Then again, it doesn't matter how we get the story as long as the truth comes out in the end. If there was a scandalous exposé that made the world a better place, or revealed something terrible we should know about, like lead in the drinking water in Flint, Michigan, I wouldn't care who revealed it; I'd just want to know. I'd want everyone to know because it's their right.

We walk into the grand ballroom at about ten, and the event is already in full swing. Diane abandons me fairly quickly, heading off to schmooze with people whose company is past my pay grade despite my moment of glory. I head to the bar to get something other than the champagne the waiters are parading around with on trays.

It's another hotel party, but this one takes place in the kind of ballroom you've probably never been granted access to. I wasn't, until I achieved a certain perceived level of success. High ceilinged affairs with imported tiles for the floor. Most conference rooms in hotels are carpeted because of the acoustics, but no one cares about that here. They want their words to carry because here is a party where people are meant to show off and be seen.

In industry parties like this, if you're in attendance, you matter. If no one sees your face, you're either too important to show up yourself or your career's on a downward arc. Either way, no one's talking about you nicely if your face isn't in the crowd.

In Hollywood, it's worse to be not spoken of. At least your name's floating around the room, pointing to relevance, if people are ripping you to shreds.

Part film festival, part Oscar after-party, part trade show, there are tables and sort of exhibitions set up along the walls where people are showing various installations. If you're important, or an insider, you're there to be pitched to. Otherwise, you're there to pretend to listen as other people pitch their ideas and concepts to you.

I'll be pitching ideas to producers, directors, moguls, whoever I think can help my career or the magazine's profile.

Diane will be there taking pitches from people wanting to work at the magazine. It's all a great big food chain. Everyone's trying to take a bite from whoever's ass is above theirs and latch on as well as they can.

A few celebrities mill about, dragged by their friends to help entice producers and directors and media moguls to latch onto the pitches, but their bored expressions really aren't helping.

Of course, no one gets close to the ridiculously expensive spread on the buffet table. Caviar, shrimp, fancy little *vol-au-vents* that probably cost a hundred dollars for barely a mouthful and took an inordinate amount of fussing over by a stressed out chef to make sit lonely and growing lukewarm. What a waste of food, not to mention carbon. It's not like those ingredients were just lying around in someone's kitchen; more likely, they were flown in from the regions they are renowned for. I wonder what happens to expensive spreads like that at the end of the night. Do the caterers get to take them home, or are they tossed out like the excess in fast foods and supermarkets? The latter are becoming more self-aware and have realized that donating it to homeless shelters and food banks is a solution, but crab cakes and *canapés* have a very "let them eat cake" sort of feel.

I wait, watching the table, getting excited when someone walks up to it, but it's only to deposit an empty glass before striding away.

So close.

I've noticed this while going to haughty parties. The higher class it is, the more expensive the food, but few people actually eat it. My first couple of events I didn't care—I'd never tasted such expensive caviar and there was no point letting it go to waste, so I'd partaken. But aberrant behavior is clocked and noted at places like these. If not by the hosts, then the people the host employs, and word gets around. You get pegged as an outsider and my actually eating the food didn't go unnoticed. Diane gave me shit about "my behavior" at work on Monday. She hadn't even been at the party in question but word travels quickly in bitchy little industry events.

How ridiculous. Other than two other girls who ate—but purged their stomachs later in the bathroom—it was just going to waste. I couldn't believe how silly and wasteful it was. But perception is everything here. It's the reason I started trying to acquire a taste for champagne. If anyone in certain circles deigns to buy or acquire you a drink, you swallow it.

There's a lot of swallowing of another kind behind closed doors, but I've never been coerced into any of that. Maybe the men can see in my eyes that I'm not as easy as the last girl. Maybe I fall too far outside the mold of the girls they're used to getting blowjobs from.

Good. I like being able to surprise people when they underestimate me. Some of them might be shocked and scandalized by the things I've done, but that's a secret that's mine alone and gives me an edge when dealing with men who truly believe they're above me.

The knowledge that I could bring them to their knees with nothing more than my imagination, sexuality, and will makes it easier to keep the pleasant smile on my face.

Drink in hand, I do a slow meander around the perimeter, checking out the films that are playing on laptops set up on tables. People don't have the attention span for a verbal pitch anymore, so it's become increasingly common to see mini-trailers made, as it were, to give an even better idea of the final product. It's a great way to tell if a certain pitch would be able to stay cost effective, or if it falls flat without major special effects.

These days, actors cost more money than they ever have, especially with the women demanding transparency and equal pay. Entitled bitches/sarcasm. It makes me sick that we are still undervalued in the entertainment industry, but we've still got a long way to go before we reach true equality.

That's part of the reason I still want to make my own films where women aren't props or bimbos or only there to make a middle-aged man seem attractive and heroic. We need better roles. Something substantive and meaty that matters.

Wait a minute.

I know those curls.

Warmth slips through my core as I remember the last time I saw Dominick only a few days ago. He squints when he sees me, but his smile is hesitant.

I never did call him, though he left me his cell number. What can I say, I got busy. Then again, I might not be averse to a repeat of that night. I keep my approach slow and steady, letting the group of businessmen ahead of me move along so I arrive in front of Dominick alone.

"Hey stranger," he says. "Long time, no see."

"Indeed. What's a guy like you doing in a place like this?" I spin the old joke.

He smiles and pats the monitor beside him. "Working."

"You're a filmmaker?"

He shrugs a shoulder. "Looks like it."

I focus on the screen, at first politely, then forgetting about him as the images take over.

Bodies move sinuously, a close-up, skin rubbing skin like a pit of snakes. But there's a strange sort of overlay to the screen, not quite translucent. More like static that washes the screen with a paleness that almost obliterates the bodies.

And there are flickers of something in the film, staying on the screen just longer than subliminal advertisements would be seen, images of blood spilling and needles being plunged into bodies, and babies with faces scrunched up bawling.

And a whip slapping out to tear through a leaf. Shots of a jungle. A compound inside the jungle, but more like a gated community where you can tell from the ornate gates that it houses true wealth. All these flash across the screen.

But always back to the sensual bodies.

I frown. "Where is this?"

"Central America."

*Belize, maybe?* "What is it? You made it?"

He nods. "I did."

"What is that place?" I shiver, an almost superstitious chill running through me like I've seen it before and forgotten.

He leans close before smiling. "It's fictional, Catherine. A set. The story is one I'm trying to get picked up."

"What is that place? It feels..." Dangerous, sexy, interesting... I'm not sure which word to choose.

"It's more abstract at the moment, as I'm going for showcasing the vibe rather than the plot."

"But..." I trail off, feeling stupid. It felt so...real. "You invoked a real sense of authenticity," I say, taking a sip of my drink.

"Thank you. Anything that gets their asses in the chair, right?"

"I have heard that said once or twice. Sex sells."

"That it does. Speaking of...are you here alone tonight?" His eyes wander over my body, making me glow with heat beneath my cobalt blue dress. "Tell me why you broke up with your ex. The one with the amazing cock."

No one's close enough to hear us, and I get a dirty little thrill talking about this shit surrounded by people pitching serious political news stories. I lean in nice and close. "Well, I discovered my sexy boyfriend was cheating on me by finding his overnight sex bag he hid in his car trunk. I stole the condoms and put pepper oil in the lube bottle."

Dominick's eyes light up. "You're kind of an evil genius."

"Tell me something personal."

He rattles the ice cubes around in his empty glass. "I can't imagine having sex while being sober. I don't remember fucking while being in true love—mutually, I should add. I haven't been sexually abused, but my best lovers have and I think I'm ruined for life because now I can't be satisfied by an emotionally healthy and nice girl that likes to make missionary love." He leans closer. "Your turn."

"If my parents weren't still alive, I would be completely selfish and be living the life of a cliché drug addict. I would party till I overdosed and I might even have fake tits. I would definitely be sluttier. I wouldn't give a fuck."

"This conversation makes me wish bad things upon your parents."

My pussy throbs. *Hungry bitch.* I love the way Dominick flirts. It makes me want to blow this off and go home with him.

He'd take me and fuck me and it would be amazing.

But I'm not up for that tonight. I'd rather a new adventure instead of a repeat performance, as good as he was in bed. "Unfortunately this is a strictly professional event. I'm here with the boss."

"Ah, duty calls. Let me know if you need rescuing again. I liked that a lot last time."

Incorrigible. I smile. "She's a better date than my last one. But, I should get going. I'm on the clock."

He grins. "So am I."

"See you around, Dominick."

"Count on it, Catherine." Some people can make the syllables of your name sound exotic and tantalizing. Dominick is one of those people.

I'm here to work, though, and so for the next half an hour or so, I make a few pitches to major networks and syndicates on behalf of the magazine. I also do my best to promote my own work, as right now I'm under an exclusive contract with the magazine, so where my work goes, they get a pound of flesh. It behooves them for me to do well on my own as well. Really, it's a good incentive for their employees to make their own opportunities.

I'm just shaking the hand of a major network producer and giving him my card when I see Colleen Masterman—legendary director. To say this moment knocks the wind out of me is an understatement— she's been one of my idols since I was a teenager. Not so much when it comes to content, but the woman is an inspiration to girls who saw nothing but men dominating the field.

I stride up to her and wait for a lull in the conversation. She turns toward me. "And you are?"

I hand her my card, unable to form words, afraid I'll say something inane.

She nods. "Ah, yes. I remember something about the porn star you wrote about. Amanda Luna."

"Inana Luna," I correct her, a little more sharply than I intended to, but I'm tense over her mischaracterization and condescension. I clear my throat. "And she was an artist, a provocateur, not a porn star. She never did porn."

Her smile is brittle, put on for those around us. "However you want to dress it up, dear. Anyways, what have you been working on since then?"

I can't keep my mouth shut, so I add, "And if she had been a porn star, would that be a problem? This city bores and breeds them, it's part of our culture and lure."

One of the men beside her tries to soften my tone, breaking the tension. "Haven't you heard? Catherine here did the Duncan piece. It was quite sensational. kudos, young lady." He raises his glass to me.

I nod my thanks, hackles smoothed a little. He's good, must work in PR to be able to pour it on like a tap.

Colleen grimaces, hiding it with a sip of champagne. "Ah, yes. Too bad you didn't get Duncan's side of the story before he was arrested. That would have made it truly fabulous."

She's right, that would have been an amazing addition to the interview, but there wasn't time. Benny had left from our meeting and gone back to the police station to turn in more information.

"It would have, time permitting. The client wasn't able to—"

She laughs. "It's not about what they're able to do. It's about getting the story, the best story in every situation. Fiction, memoir, nonfiction, the narrative should always be as streamlined and fascinating and whole as we can make it. Maybe next time you'll remember that."

I nod, a little shell-shocked by her rudeness, but none of the people around her seem to notice. I guess this is how she always is.

I swallow hard. "Anyways, I was hoping for a moment of your time to ask your opinion on something?"

She arches a brow and turns to the young man standing next to her.

She's bored and moves on before my lips can close around the taste of her dismissal.

The woman I've looked up to for so many years doesn't even have a moment to spare for an actual meaningful conversation. Fair enough if she were busy, but she's not. She just sized me up and instantly came to the conclusion that I am a person she is somehow required to hate and forget.

It's like finding out Santa is real but he scornfully informs you that the letters you sent him were trite and inane with sloppy hand-writing.

I'm so sick of female-on-female distain. This is so much more than an impartial rejection, and that's what stings the most.

I head back to the bar, get a drink, and head for the balcony to get some air. I'd love to go grab a car home, but it would be unprofessional for me to leave this early. I should go pitch some more ideas, try to impress the right people with my stunning repartee, but at the moment I feel nothing but crushed. The fact I care so much about one person's opinion also adds a tinge of the pathetic to my emotional cocktail, leaving a bitter taste on my tongue.

Diane's going to be pissed at me squandering precious time on my phone here.

Mr. X: *How's your night going?*

Me: *Not amazing.*

Mr. X: *Why not?*

I sigh. It seems stupid to tell him because he's a stranger. But sometimes it's easier to talk to strangers because of the emotional distance.

Me: *I met Colleen Masterman. My idol since I was fifteen and one of the reasons I went into film school.*

Mr. X: *That's amazing. But I'm sensing it didn't go well?*

Me: *Not at all. She was not what I expected.*

Mr. X: *She didn't want to hang out trading cute little anecdotes and dishing industry dirt?*

Me: *Exactly. I looked up to her so much. There aren't many female directors and even though her movies weren't always my favorite, she made me think I could be there too someday, before I settled with print.*

Mr. X: *At the risk of sounding crass, sometimes women are worse than men in the way they treat each other. They worry that they'll show favoritism to other girls and so they overcompensate by being total cunts to others instead of helping them. Reaching back to bring others forward, as it were. It's not right, but it is what it is. I bet she felt threatened by you.*

Me: *Threatened? Why?*

Mr. X: *You're younger than her, smarter than her, and being talked about more than her right now. Add to that the fact you're also more beautiful than her, it's no wonder she was aloof.*

Me: *I doubt that, but thank you for trying to frame her rejection.*

Mr. X: *I'm serious. I could have told you that she'd be a bitch if you approached her. This one time, she had an intern fired for wearing the same dress as her to a premiere. She's an ice queen through and through. Don't worry about her. You want to get under her skin, send her a basket of flowers with a card that says, Happy Retirement.*

That earns a smile. I relax and maybe that's what allows the memory of Dominick's pitch video to slither back into my mind. The thing is, it felt very Juliette Society and I've come to suspect Mr. X is also a part of it, but I can't outright ask him. I can't go back to Dominick and ask him that either as that's not something you casually bring up in conversation. Besides, sometimes it's best to have a secret in your pocket. So if Dominick is in TJS, then I'll know that he is, but he won't know that I know.

Instead, I text Mr. X: *What do you know about Central America?*

I hedge, gambling with the location. I could be wrong, but Dominick's video looked like Belize or Honduras. My grade school teacher went on a trip to Belize once, and it looked close but I could be way off.

His reply takes a moment, a long time actually, as I realize my drink is empty, he finally responds.

Mr. X: *I'm assuming you're talking about Honduras. I can't tell you but I can show you if you're interested in learning more...*

Honduras! Excellent confirmation from him.

Me: *As much as I appreciate the offer, I don't really have time for a vacation right now...especially with someone I've never met in person.*

I want to add "no offense," but his offer is coming off as strange and inappropriate. I've never even heard his voice on a call, never mind seen the man.

At least I'm assuming Mr. X is a man. Behind a text, anyone could be sending the words I've been reading. But Dominick and Benny both referred to Mr. X as "he," so I think it's safe to presume.

Mr. X: *You misunderstand. This isn't a vacation. There's a conference there, that's all, reminiscent of the G8 though not quite the same. But it could be a great follow-up to your last article. I know something that would make the last one seem as scandalous as a church picnic.*

Me: *I've heard about some pretty scandalous church picnics.*

I don't send a winky face but he knows I'm kidding.

Mr. X: *I bet you have. But nothing like this. Are you interested?*

My pulse kicks up again. Is this the part where he cashes in on the goodwill he's given me so far? What's the price of his favors?

Me: *Show me how?*

Mr. X: *A business trip, of course. I have got a private jet, if you're worried about the cost at this moment.*

The cost is a factor, but it's not my biggest reticence. The situation is still more than a little strange.

Me: *Is there an expiration date to this? When is the conference?*

Mr. X: *Soon. So let me know if you want to participate ASAP.*

It doesn't escape my attention that he didn't actually give me a date. Is he trying to keep me on my toes, unsettled, unsteady? I'm not going to be rushed into making a decision, and I've been the recipient of power plays more subtle and effective than this.

Me: *I appreciate the offer. I'll let you know.*

His offer is crossing a line into inappropriate territory. I also don't want to burn a potentially important interview. I search online, and I find it. Honduras has been selected as the location for a yearly eco conference. Political and environmental leaders from around the world will be present, some who are quite controversial and profit-driven.

# SEVEN

CERTAIN PLACES FEEL INNATELY WRONG when they're empty. When everyone's gone home and the lights go off, things change dramatically. Grocery stores, bars and clubs, schools. A lot of horror movies use this to their advantage, playing upon the jarring discord between our expectations of a place and the settings they choose. Places we expect to see bustling with people and life become unsettling when they're suddenly emptied and quiet. The sound and activity fade out, leaving room for a more atmospheric opportunity for unease to creep in. Why are they empty? What happened?

Picture yourself walking into a stadium, waiting for a football game or a concert—and you're the only one there.

Or maybe you rush through the departures entrance at an airport, too caught up in thoughts of missing your flight to notice there are no cars or other people, and you walk in the door only to be greeted with silence.

Maybe you walk inside a shopping mall and instead of the food court being filled with the sounds of hundreds of people and scents of different mall foods for sale, there's nothing but the echoes of your footfalls on the floor, reverberating slightly in the still, cool air.

I don't know about you, but I'd be creeped out, wondering what was wrong with the place, what had happened to all the people I expected to find.

What I didn't know about that everyone else did that made them leave.

If you're the only one headed in one direction and the other side of the road headed the other way is jammed with traffic, it kind of makes you question your decision—or wonder what is happening that you don't know about. It's usually something innocuous, but sometimes there's a disaster you didn't hear about because you were listening to your music—or silence—instead of the radio and missed an important alert.

There's a name for this feeling, you know, but you probably haven't heard of it. Kenopsia. It's actually defined as follows: "*n.* the eerie, forlorn atmosphere of a place that's usually bustling with people but is now abandoned and quiet—a school hallway in the evening, an unlit office on a weekend, vacant fairgrounds—an emotional after-image that makes it seem not just empty but hyper-empty, with a total population in the negative, who are so conspicuously absent they glow like neon signs."

It's one of those perfect words that capture a specific emotion so well it makes you want to grasp the meaning in both hands and never let it go because for that moment, you feel understood. Someone got how you were feeling so well they made a definition for it.

But the word is too niche, and you eventually forget it because other than displaying your pedantry at cocktail parties, your brain has no use for the word and lets it slip away with the song lyrics you learned for the school play back in kindergarten.

But the emotion doesn't fade away the same way, particularly this specific one. I mean, we've all seen the horror movies that take place in malls, though that's more of a plot device so characters can hole up in a place with resources and, because of the size, both privacy from other survivors and the ability for isolation (which brings opportunity for danger). This emotion is one that many directors employ to play up an unnerving atmosphere.

I'm seeing a lot of parallels tonight.

My date and I are alone in the restaurant except for the efficient wait staff who are only here when we need a refill of the best champagne he ordered a bottle of. I hate champagne but am going along with it because I'm used to adapting to elitist culture when I have to put my game face on for work. It's definitely a strike against him, not asking me what I wanted to drink, instead assuming I'd be impressed and happy to go with the most expensive thing in the house.

He rented out the restaurant so we have it to ourselves. I'm flattered, but it's ostentatious and unnecessary if he's trying to win points back from the last time he took me out. And having no other diners around to observe and take the focus off of each other, the whole set-up feels forced, like one of those one-on-one dates on reality dating programs. That, and the fact that it feels like we're eating in a haunted restaurant doesn't exactly add to the ambiance.

I'm not saying this date is a horror show, but it's definitely not the experience I was hoping for when I gave Jacob another chance when he called me up and invited me on another date since he "lost me at the party." Initially I was reluctant, as he hadn't seemed to notice and didn't get in touch with me for a full week after I went home with Dominick, but eventually I said yes. I was getting overwhelmed by the flower deliveries as his means of apology…and running out of vases.

And, to be honest, I'd crept his Instagram, and there was a picture of me and all these other quotes about excitement and new adventures and hope and it was very flattering.

The thing is, it feels manufactured. Something simple and heartfelt was what I was hoping for instead of what's feeling more and more clichéd. That's the problem I have with those reality dating shows where they take contestants on these magical luxury dates in the hopes that the women—or men—will fall for the person they're all fighting for.

Sure, maybe some people do develop genuine feelings for the person, but can you really be into a stranger enough to want to marry them on the first date? If so, you're not in love with them, you're in love with the idea of them. I'm not saying genuine feelings can't develop after initial lust or attraction, but let's be honest. You don't know the person that early on. And the producers know that too; it's why they work the competitive aspect of the show so hard, encouraging envy and pitting contestants against each other so it's more about winning instead of finding a connection—though that's certainly an overused buzzword.

Most women fall in love with the experience and imprint those feelings onto the guy they're with instead of analyzing whether or not they're actually in love. And it's not only the women—the man feels pressure to fall for one of the contestants when really, maybe his match isn't on the show. She's probably not. But they wedge themselves into a relationship on an unrealistic timeline and then everyone's sad (but not surprised) when after the show ends the couple's pictures are on the cover of various supermarket tabloids with "Why they split" and "The Romance Is Over" written in bold font.

I've read studies that show if you do something exciting with someone on a first date, you're more likely to fall in love because of the chemical rush in your body. Your brain interprets it as falling in love, and you get attached more quickly. So, I guess, if you're looking to force a timeline, it's best to go for an adrenaline rush. That explains why a lot of those dating shows outings involve zip lines and bungee jumping.

The better to fool you with.

It makes sense then, that the contestants are falling for the experience instead of the bachelor or bachelorette. It's all about the fantasy, carefully cultivated until they forget that back home there won't be helicopter rides to exotic dates on mountaintops, or giant mansions to sleep in. They don't want them to remember that back home you'll be working instead of sitting around discussing your potential husband's dreamy attributes with seven of your closest frenemies, making him seem more desirable. They forget that there won't be a big swimming pool to lounge by, or private dates where your favorite band plays just for you.

So I find it even more insulting that Jacob's clearly trying to win me over with more toys and gifts and flashy crap I don't care about. What would have impressed me more would have been if he'd remembered the drink I'd ordered for myself at the bar he took me to on our first night and *asked* me if I wanted one of those instead of gloating about the quality of the champagne.

It would have impressed me more if he'd asked what I wanted to eat instead of informing me that he'd had the restaurant prepare Kobe beef steaks he'd specifically had flown in just for the occasion. I hate when people do that as though wanting praise for making a show of themselves. I don't want to fall all over myself with effusive praise for something I never wanted and don't care to have.

It's no longer in my nature to coddle phonies. I swore I'd be true to myself after Jack and I intend to keep that promise. It's also not in my nature to be outright rude, so I take this for what it is—an experience—and sip my champagne, now knowing I don't even like it if it's perfectly chilled and poured from a ridiculously overpriced vintage. At least now I can say I've drunk some.

"Good, huh?" Jacob asks, swallowing more.

I make a non-committal noise and set my glass down.

"I'm glad you finally saw sense and agreed to come out with me. Most girls would have caved way earlier."

"I am not most girls, then," I say archly.

He winks. "I find most girls are basically the same at the end of the day."

Way to actually insult me. "When does it become acceptable to say things like this to people?"

He grins. "I'm just kidding." His smile fades when he notices I'm not buying the charm. "Hey, I'm sorry, okay? You made me nervous. You're an intimidating woman, Catherine."

I don't buy it, but I relax a little. What's the tax bracket that leads you to believe people are things to acquire instead of to interact with and care about? Now I get it. He only pursued me because I resisted. He's used to girls falling all over themselves when he snaps his fingers. No wonder he was interested in me. I present a challenge to his monstrous ego.

"I'll take that as a compliment, Jacob."

"You should. Man, I had a crazy week last week." He leans back, waiting for me to ask what his crazy week entailed.

"Oh?" One syllable is the most I can scrape together relatively free of sarcasm.

"Yeah."

Drawing out information you don't really care about is difficult. "So what was so wild about last week?"

"Well, it was busy. I was doing research, I guess how you do for your work."

"What were you researching?" I ask.

"I bought a new car."

My phone buzzes, and I glance at the screen, not feeling bad about it—Jacob's phone has been in his hand the whole date. It's a text from Dominick, but I don't answer it. At least one of us should maintain a standard of civility and politeness on this date. I turn my phone off without reading the text. "What kind of car did you get?"

"A Ferrari."

"What was wrong with the Lambo?"

He shrugs. "I've had it for a while."

"People have seen you in it. How embarrassing!" How gauche.

He laughs, but it's definitely forced and I feel chastened at poking fun when I know he's insecure and tries to cover it with flashy things.

"What color did you get?" I ask as a peace offering. "I really liked the color of your last car, it was very unique."

He visibly perks up. "It's sort of a pearlescent gray. Custom."

"Nice. I saw one the other day that changed from purple to green, though I'm not sure how they do that." But all I can think is, wrong choice of color.

"I thought of doing that, but I've seen three like that. I wanted something different."

"How do you know it was three cars and not the same car three times?"

He takes a sip of champagne. "I don't, I guess."

The conversation stalls and my phone buzzes again.

"Do you need to get that?" he asks.

I shake my head.

"Ronny? Hey, how's it going?" He answers his own phone, cutting off my next sentence: *That would be rude of me to talk to someone else in front of you while on a date.*

And yet, I get a front row seat to his bragging about his success and new car. It's his father's success, not his, and my patience is wearing down to the nubs. Bragging is a turn-off at best. This is even worse.

This is the last time I go along with a date because I'm procrastinating with my work. Maybe I'm not the exact same person I was when I started out, but I've been trying to stay humble as I grow into this insane world. Keeping the balance of normal and the other more wealthy people I co-exist with is a challenge. When you're immersed in a certain lifestyle for long enough, you start picking things up.

Vocabulary, habits, attitudes. Hell, even hairstyles.

No matter the people I'm around, no matter the things I do and see, I'm going to make damn sure that I die as myself and not some pretender. Not some phony.

I abandon my champagne for water, savoring the chill of the ice while he continues his call, ignoring me once again, only this time it feels worse because there's no one else to talk to. Being ignored in a room full of people stings less than being ignored when it's just you two.

# EIGHT

I'M OUT OF THE UBER and heading up to my entrance when I notice Dominick is waiting at my place. My steps halt a little, but I keep walking.

"You didn't answer my texts," he says.

To be honest, I'd forgotten all about them, what with trying to let Jacob down gently—an interesting task since he only seems to care about pursuing me when I'm not interested. Telling him I just wanted to be friends got his attention and suddenly made him want me again. But I gave him two chances, which was more than enough disappointment. It's the best thing for us both in the long run.

He needs to be with someone who's impressed by his things. Of course, that's when the few employees in the restaurant chose to come and watch the show he put on, trying to woo me.

He continued to pursue me and I was trying to be polite, but there's no right way to tell a guy you're not into it. They will always be shattered. This is from the mouth of a guy friend of mine. I asked him for advice on how to deal with a friendly guy who I told I was not looking to be more than friends with and he said, that is basically like telling a guy, never in a million years would I fuck you. It's a punch in the gut and there's no way to soften the blow.

Jacob may not have cared about actually courting me, but his ego would still be bruised. So I tore the bandage off firmly to be as kind as I could and got out of there quickly after. I doubt Jacob's seriously going to be sad about us not working out. He never cared to begin with. He'd mentioned an ex. And it became clear that he was either only trying to use me to get over her, or use me to make her jealous. Either way I was being used.

I'm no pawn. I don't want to be a part of his game. I just wanted sex.

And now, here's a man who knows how to give it to me.

"Good evening to you too, Dominick."

"Where were you tonight?"

The possessiveness in his voice annoys me, but also kind of perks me up. He's a bit alpha, which really turns me on after the night I've had. "Out."

"Obviously."

I'm not sure if it's a game he's playing, acting out a role of jealous boyfriend, or if he's actually come to be possessive over me in such a short time, but I open the door and swing it wide enough that he can follow me inside if he chooses.

I like that glint in his eye.

There are no words when we get in the elevator together and ride it up to my floor. No words as we get inside. No words as we head to my bedroom and one by one, we strip out of our clothes, eyeing each other up like predator and prey but in this room right now there are only predators—and no praying.

Maybe he'll scream out, "Oh, god," by the time this is over. Maybe I will.

He wraps his arms around me, and I soak up the heat of his chest against mine for a moment before I scratch my nails down his back. He shivers and pulls back enough to look me in the eyes when he cups my ass and squeezes it hard enough I can still feel his fingers there when he moves them up my back, kneading as he goes.

I thrust my tongue into his mouth and grind against his hips, smiling against his mouth when he goes from semi-hard to ragingly hard against me.

Funny how you can fuck every day and before his cock enters you, it feels like it's been forever since the last time. I pull him down to the bed on top of me. He tugs on my hair, nipping the outline of my jaw with his teeth, but then backs away and teases me with the tip of his tongue on the hollow of my throat.

I'm already growing weary of cat and mouse, and I hook a leg across his and shove the blanket out of my way, annoyed at the little tangle getting in my way of a great time.

He reaches between us and I look him in the eyes, waiting for him to discover that I'm soaked. I have been since we got in the elevator.

He bites his lip and lets out a moan. I get it. It's fucking hot knowing you've made someone wet as fuck. He pushes two fingers inside me, stroking me at a leisurely pace that opens up my tight little hole and has me shuddering for more, but he pulls them out and slathers my come all over my clit, rubbing swift little circles that make me gasp and clench. Again he pulls away at the penultimate moment.

I pull his hair for making me wait.

And then I rub my pussy as well and get my hand nice and wet before using my lube to stroke his fat cock up and down.

He retaliates by positioning his cock at my entrance and slipping just inside, just the tip, and caressing my tits, pinching the nipples with his slippery fingers like he's milking me.

I want his cream in me.

I let my knees fall open like a butterfly, and slightly pull back, letting him chase me with his hips if he wants to stay inside. Like a good boy, he does.

Oh, god, he does.

He slides in and out of me and I'm so fucking wet I can feel it dripping down to my asshole and onto the bed. Maybe it's his pre-come too, but I'm caught up in the silky texture of it and just want more.

But I want to feel this in other positions too, so I push at his chest and flip over when he pulls out so he can take me from behind.

I bend my knees and brace with my hips and diddle myself with my fingers in the space I've created between my clit and the bed while he rams into me from behind, his hips making little smacking sounds against my ass, his hands squeezing my thighs, flank, back, shoulder.

This is what I want forever. Fighting with my body with someone who knows what he's doing to make me feel so present and good. I want someone to let me be whoever I need to be to get off the best. Let me be strong, let me be weak, don't judge me for wanting what I want or sometimes for not knowing in the moment what that is until it happens.

He moves harder and faster and then we're up against the wall and my head knocks against it as he pounds into me and the way it hurts is brutally perfect. If he stops doing it I'll scratch his back until it bleeds.

My orgasm dances just out of reach, and I spread my legs as wide as I can. He holds my hands above my head, and my nipples rub against the sheets, heating with the friction of the movement of our hips. I can feel my belly start to tighten, and tension building deep inside, and his hands clench mine once before releasing them and digging into my hips, using me to jerk back onto his cock and meet his every thrust. I bury my face in the pillow, hard enough to smother my moans when my pussy clenches around his cock like a vise grip.

He shudders and his hot jets of come squirt into me, basting my insides with his juices before he collapses on top of me.

"How was it that good?" he says a few minutes later.

"I don't know," I reply, wondering when he'll leave so I can take a bath and imagine what my next encounter will be like. Who it will be with.

"I wouldn't be averse to doing this again. A lot."

Damn. Two "it's not you, it's me" speeches in one night. Banner night on the relationship front. He was alpha out of jealousy over me being on a date. That means he's going to want to be exclusive soon. "Dominick, you're a great guy, but I need to focus on my career right now."

"Is that you saying you don't want to see me again?"

I shake my head. "I'm not looking to be locked down right now. I did that before and it's not for me. It may never be, I'm not sure."

"I can't be what you need?" He sits up.

"We're similar in a lot of ways. We're compatible, even." I think of his film and love that he'd understand art and the muse and artistic expression. "Your art is admirable. We just want different things right now."

"I see. Fair enough." He dresses and leaves. I don't offer to let him stay the night, and he doesn't ask if he can. We both know the score.

The game is over between us.

# NINE

THEY SAY WHEN YOU DIE, your life flashes before your eyes.

Maybe sometimes that's the case. Maybe if you see it coming.

The knife swooping at you in a graceful arc.

The flash of the muzzle of the gun.

Hands tightening around your neck.

An airplane plummeting to the ground as gravity pulls your body up against the seatbelt.

Maybe then your brain has time to flip a switch into that mode of reminiscence and looking back. Not me.

I don't get a neat, little montage of moments that are rife with poignancy or regret. I don't get much of anything when the vehicle slams into mine, T-boning me from the passenger's side, closer to the rear than the front, except for a slow motion blur of everything outside my car. It takes longer than I'd imagined for the world to stop spinning—I even have time to think, *What the hell just happened? Why am I spinning? This feels like the tea cup ride*, before the stench of burning rubber fills my nostrils. When the world stops moving, I lift my head from the steering wheel, blinking hard to focus.

I'd gag on the acrid smell, but then the pain hits and I can't focus on anything but the sharpness of it, the way it slices through everything else and cuts my world down to nothing but sensations. Pain is singularly jealous in the way it wants us to think of nothing else. A reboot to the system that can't be denied, wiping away your very existence for a moment until all there is, is the hurt. Yet somehow we manage.

Large hands pull me away from the steering wheel, leaning me back into my seat as a cloth is pressed against my forehead. A napkin?

"Don't move, honey. I've already called an ambulance, and they're on their way," a man says in a Boston accent.

I put my hand on the cloth, waving his away. "What happened?" I ask, still dazed from the impact. "Is the other driver okay?"

"I was eating on the patio. He hit you and ran like a coward, didn't even stop to see if you were okay. He was probably worried he'd killed you."

I open the door and swing my legs out.

"Careful, honey. I don't think you should be walking around right now."

"I'm okay." I head to the passenger side and take in the state of my car. It's definitely a write-off, but you could tell I was fine on my side. More likely, the driver was probably scared shitless and fled the scene because he didn't have insurance. I did an article about it, and learned that about twelve percent of drivers have no insurance. In this economy, some bills simply can't be paid, and it's tragic and sad that in a country as great as America, things like this are happening where people are forced to choose between not luxuries but necessities on a routine basis.

Then again, insurance companies are some of the biggest scammers around. Don't even get me started on medical insurance and the highly unethical things happening there. Maybe that should be my next big story. Then again, it's not exactly a shock that a giant corporation is evil.

"Miss?" The man frowns and I realize I've been sitting here, probably with my eyes glazed over, while I ponder possible stories to write about.

I didn't even see a vehicle coming at me. I need to focus. "What was he driving?"

My good Samaritan shrugs. "I don't know, a Volvo or something. I was more worried about the blood dripping down your face after I called 911."

I pull the napkin away and feel a tiny trickle down my face again. That's going to need a stitch. I look in the rear view mirror, but other than the blood that was spilled, which makes it look worse than it is, it's just a small nick near my hairline that's bleeding like a pig. "I think I need a couple stitches, but I'm okay."

The paramedics pull up what feels like a second later, but my sense of time is off as my phone shows it's been over ten minutes.

Although it was my car that was hit, I'm the one who feels like I was smashed into. No bruises have formed yet, but they're there, migrating from my bones up through my tissues and skin and they'll make an appearance in a couple of days.

I don't seem to be concussed or have whiplash, though my neck is sore. I've had worse, but I move slowly to the bathroom. It's funny how you take things like good health and mobility for granted until something goes wrong and you're injured and every step goes from automatic to awkward. My back muscles protest as I fill the bathtub with water as hot as I can stand it and dump in a bunch of Epsom salts, swirling them around the bottom of the tub to dissolve away. The heat of the water makes me wince as much as the movements it takes getting in, but soon I'm surrounded by the heat. Sweat forms on my face and makes my forehead sting near the stitches, but since that's the worst I walked away with, I'm counting blessings as I blot my lip.

There's a place. Muggy and humid, filled with everything you could imagine.

Some say you have to die to get there. Others say you only get there by really living.

*Carpe diem*, as it were, but closer to *carpe noctem*. Seize the night.

I'm walking through a pathway obscured by plants with huge, soft leaves I've never seen before except in pictures. I stop and stick my fingernail through one of them to see if it's real. The plant winces and milky tears that smell like sex ooze down to the ground, waves rippling out like drops in a puddle when they land, except it's in the dirt.

A snake slithers by, green, black, shiny. I follow it with my eyes as its stomach bunches and relaxes and pulls it forward. I'm drawn forward in its strangely hypnotic wake, warm and curious as to where it's going to lead me.

There's a break in the path, and through it, the terracotta hue of a stuccoed wall comes into sight. I've seen it before, but where? I know there's something behind that wall I need to get to, only I can't quite remember what it is.

A bright red flower appears when I pull a low-hanging leaf out of the way, and I pause to marvel at the strange shapes of the petals, so unlike the blossoms I'm used to.

I inhale deeply, and the stench of rot assails my nostrils, making me gag. I pull back and the snake strikes my foot.

Poison spreads from the bite and courses through my veins at the speed of my beating heart.

But I know, somehow, that I'll be okay.

I come to with a start, neck stiff, in cold water, the remnants of my dream dissolving away before I can analyze it. Something about Dominick's video...the compound I saw... But it's gone. I pull the plug with my toe and reach for the towel, pausing to stare at my fingers.

Apparently, our fingers wrinkle when we get them wet because the puckers and folds give them a better grip. Mine are brutal. How long was I asleep?

I'm lucky I didn't slide beneath the surface and drown.

On the plus side, I'm still breathing. On the negative, it looks like I was not as free of concussion as I thought. It's jarring losing time like that, sort of like I ceased to exist for a while. Maybe I did.

Maybe we do. Are we more than our bodies? Are we our consciousness? Because if so, what happens to us when we sleep? The French say that the orgasm is the little death. I think it's when you're in a dead sleep. Orgasms are when you're the most slammed into your body and aware of it. I wrap a towel around myself and head straight for bed, not trusting or wanting anything but sleep.

# TEN

CONSCIOUSNESS EASES UPON ME, warm and damp like the towel that's still encasing my torso. Unfortunately, it's spread its wetness to the sheets. I grimace and sit up, wincing as my head protests the change in elevation with a few sick throbs. Somehow it feels soft, like an overripe piece of fruit being squeezed.

I brew some coffee, hoping at least part of the headache is a direct result of lack of caffeination, and go get dressed in panties and a tank top, not bothering with more than that. The headache passes with some deep breaths and a few gulps of coffee, so I grab my phone to face the day.

I've got one hundred and thirty seven missed texts.

Forty-nine new voicemails.

The last one is from my brother, telling me to turn on the television. My heart starts pounding as I head for the remote, different catastrophes playing through my mind.

The JFK assassination.

The Columbine shooting.

9/11.

Orlando.

News affects us all differently, but when big events happen, when tragedies strike, they connect us all because they remind us of our humanity. For a while, even though it never seems to last nearly long enough, we swear to do better, be better, fix the world and stop hurting each other.

But when the news strikes, people rush to their screens and then are unable to look away from what they see. The stories don't have to be filled with deaths to be compelling.

The moon landing.

The Oscars.

*I Am Cait.*

But day by day, inertia creeps back in. Indifference creeps back in and we go back to our socially acceptable levels of self-absorption. We abandon the social activism, shy away from the hashtag activism and post our selfies and meaningless first-world-problem tweets with no outraged backlash from people who have also moved on to the next thing.

But today is different. This is more like a personal tragedy unfolding in the public eye.

Of course, at the root of it, every tragedy is private. Every human has family and friends, people who loved them and will miss them when something happens, but the devastation is usually local instead of national.

Imagine turning on the television and seeing yourself.

Not because you were interviewed, or because you interviewed someone else and that was getting publicity.

Not because you were captured in the background of another story and waved for Mom.

The footage is so old it's like watching another person instead of myself, but I know it's me immediately. Whoever filmed it knew what they were doing, but I had no idea I was being filmed or that cameras were allowed in the mansion that night.

Something drew me to the mask he was wearing, so much more elaborate than the others I'd seen there. And then it hit me. He was the man from a dream I used to have, the Renaissance man in the harlequin mask who unlocked me.

He carried himself with a swagger, so cocksure and certain of his appeal. His skin was tanned and leathery but his body was taut and muscular and toned. He looked like he took care of himself, like he worked out. His physique was speaking to me and it told me that that man knew his power and how to use it. And he looked good for his age, whatever that was, in his late forties, at least.

"As you can see, some of the footage here was quite dark, but it's definitely her."

The anchorwoman drones on as I drown in memories of that night.

Then he was so close I could smell him. He smelled rich and I should have recognized his cologne. By the time he was in front of me, I was hooked. There was something about him, but I just couldn't put my finger on it at first. Then it hit me. Something about him reminded me of Jack.

Jack sometime in the future.

I'd always told myself that I wanted to grow old with Jack. Sometimes I'd liked to imagine what we'd be like when we were in our fifties or sixties, when we'd lived half a lifetime in each other's company. I'd wondered how we'd look with all that living under our belt, how we'd relate to each other, how we'd fuck.

And this guy, I decided right then and there, that he represented my fantasy of how Jack might turn out when we were older, what he'd look like, how he'd carry himself.

And I know how that sounds, even now. It sounds like an excuse, and in a way it was. It was an excuse that my brain came up with to explain the way my body was feeling. I felt an immense attraction to that man, who was a blank canvas to me, on whom I projected the fantasy I wanted. And lived it and experienced it. For real.

I'm almost offended in hindsight that I needed an excuse to do the things I wanted when I was doing them anyways. I cheated on Jack and tried to justify it by projecting my boyfriend onto this stranger. Cheating isn't something I condone. But if you're going to do things, at least don't lie to yourself about them to try to justify taking the leap. It's disingenuous.

The camera pans in so I'm the one taking up almost all of the frame. The man offers me his hand. You clearly see me take it without hesitation or reserve. Then he leads me downstairs into the main room and all the way to the end of the room, as if he's parading me in front of everybody, showing me off.

Knowing now that this was likely my first of The Juliette Society's events makes me realize he probably was—especially since someone was filming it. I feel strangely violated by this. But consent isn't just about who touches you. Secretly being filmed is disgusting and a violation because someone can watch that over and over again. It's not fair for someone to remove your consent that way, make it so they can watch themselves fucking you in perpetuity when you said yes only one time.

The camera cuts to me sitting down with my legs closed together and my hands on my lap, as prim and proper as a Catholic schoolgirl. He taps the arm of the chair and I swing my legs up over each arm of the chair and slide my butt forward to the edge of the seat. The camera cuts the part where he knelt down in front of me, took my left foot in his hands and started kneading the sole with his thumbs. It cuts how he kissed the sole of my foot, sucking on each toe, circling around and between them with his tongue.

But it shows when he puts his hands on my legs, clasps them together and lifts them up so my feet are over my head, and pussy is sticking out, wet and plump and in full view. I wrap my arms around my legs to hold them in place while he puts one hand on my thigh and gives my pussy a quick little slap with the other.

It cuts again, not showing anything with the man's face, only his hands and everything of me—everything except the parts they've blurred out on television.

The video on the internet doesn't censor anything. You can see the trail of juice dripping down to my asshole, his fingers sliding right inside, probing around the soft fleshy mound behind my clitoris. You can watch as I climb up onto the arms, crouch down and slowly lower myself onto his cock. I spit in my hand and pump it along the shaft, sheathing with saliva and juice, and keep pumping it like I'd done it a thousand times before.

But then it cuts to the part where I'm surrounded by a wall of male flesh separating me from the rest of the room, only you can still see me and everything that I'm doing. None of the men's faces or enough details to be incriminating to them, I notice resentfully.

You just see the anonymous cocks approach, and the way I grab for everything in my reach with everything that I've got. Rivers of come flooding me all over. The sheer ecstasy and hunger on my face.

And a few more shots to show that I didn't stop for quite some time.

It's devastating.

But not because I regret doing it. It's devastating because someone's using this against me, as though trying to define me by this one act I did one time in my life. They're wielding my sexuality as a weapon against me when I'm not allowed to do the same.

Hell, if they'd pan out and see who I'm fucking, they'd forget all about me and focus on DeVille. Then again, I'd become Monica Lewinsky version 2.0 and that's only going to assure this scandal gets permanently etched into the history books.

I check my emails, deleting inappropriate ones that people have sent inviting me to "make a sequel." I delete posts from my page on Facebook. But I can't do anything about the hashtag on Twitter, or the crude things people have tagged me in on Instagram.

I can't contain the story. It's already too big and out of my hands. I'm just big enough for people to want to tear me down. Tears of frustration sting my eyes.

Will my career be ruined by this the way that other women who have braved scandals were? Even if this blows over tomorrow—which it will not, this is character decimation—I'll be talked about, seen in ways I never chose to show people. It's bullshit, and anger heats my stomach. It's a good metaphor for how women enjoying sex is taboo and we can't be sexual creatures in our own right without it tainting us and making us seem less than instead. But men doing exactly the same thing get an aura of power in the same situation.

It angers me because it's unfair.

I call Diane and she picks up immediately. I'm not shocked. "Diane—"

"Save it," she cuts in. "I don't need to know the details. I need you to take a few days off, lie low and wait for the dust to settle. We're looking into who released the footage, but there's nothing so far."

"Diane, I need to tell my side of the story."

"Catherine, no one's going to listen." Her voice is gentler, but I still hear the resolve in it. In an industry where perception is every-thing, I'm fucked and need to do serious damage control.

I'm helpless to fix this. I can't refute that that is indeed me, getting my brains fucked out by more than a few men. My name is being linked to Jack, and through Jack, DeVille.

Funny how no one can tell it's him with me in the video. Then again, he was inside me there and I never noticed. The brain shows you what it wants to see, blinding you to the obvious much of the time.

It reminds me of someone else who manipulates the eye through video medium. Dominick. That bastard. I don't know how he got this video—hell, maybe he shot it himself, but this can't be a coinci-dence. I reject him and like any jilted lover, he decides to ruin my life.

Only in this case, he's not just writing angry posts on Facebook or keying my car. He's trying to ruin me.

Maybe I'm blindsided here, but I'm not powerless.

I send a text.

Me: *Are you still willing to give me that interview?*

Mr. X replies a moment later: *You're interested? You'd be leaving tomorrow.*

Me: *That's perfect. I'll gladly take you up on your offer if it's still available.*

Mr. X: *It is, but I want you to prove you're serious, so no ticket will be provided.*

Fine by me. I'm not in the mood to be at the mercy of a man's fragile ego or generosity with strings attached. Dominick can go fuck himself, and X will eat his words.

Me: *I'm deadly serious.*

Mr. X: *Regardless, I'd like you to prove it by action, not word.*

Dominick had said Mr. X liked doing things his own way.

I check my online banking and look at tickets to Honduras. If I scrape together the dregs of my savings and combine it with my air miles, I can buy the plane ticket. I'll get there a few days early for the conference to prepare and also escape from the scandal which is already taking a toll on me emotionally.

Me: *I just booked it.*

Mr. X: *Get ready for something huge. This is going to make your career.*

Right now, I'll settle for saving my career.

# ELEVEN

IT GOES WITHOUT SAYING THAT some countries are more corrupt than others. No country in the world is free of bloodshed, but some have seen more horrors than others.

You hear the horror movies say that houses are haunted because they were built on graveyards, but name me a part of America where someone hasn't died on it. Civil wars have been fought on our soil from the beginning to today and probably tomorrow as well because we never seem to learn. But it's not just America; it's the world.

I've noticed that warmer places have more violence. Maybe it's the heat and the effect it has on our primitive minds. When we were cold, we had to worry about not freezing to death and gathering enough food to outlast the winter before focusing on slaughtering the people in neighboring villages.

People used to have to either run or ride horses to war. Sure, soldiers must follow orders, but when you had to run for days, weeks, months, years to get into the fight, it took the frivolity out of it. Nowadays our leaders can kill people from the comfort of their office, sitting on their asses sipping full-fat lattes while others drop the bombs—or while the missiles launch themselves. A push of a button... So as advanced as we've become, war's definitely gotten less personal from when leaders fought on the battlegrounds with their soldiers.

I'm not sure if they'd care more or less if they were forced to witness firsthand the lives literally blown apart by their conflicts. To look the people fighting for them in the eyes and tell them to charge forward knowing all of them won't make it home. Maybe those in charge would strive harder to avoid the battles in the first place when it became that personal again.

But probably not.

War is personal for the soldiers, not the people in charge. It's personal for the civilians left standing in the rubble of their home countries wondering how the hell they'll ever rebuild from a loss greater than the scope of imagination.

Central America is about as poor as it gets as a whole. Corruption is rife, and people can't get the help they need. It's something that should anger a lot more people, knowing some are dying and mired in lives that have no hope or opportunities, but it's not news.

We already know that people need help. But then again, kids are starving and unsafe and being killed in America too.

The hotel's state is a jarring reminder of the privilege we have in America. I didn't really look ahead when I booked, but this is at about the level of an hourly motel back home. And fair enough. I'm not exactly staying in a touristy area, so this area probably has less money than others because of it. Last time I stayed at a star-rated hotel, even with my lack of experience, it was clear that five stars does not mean the same thing everywhere you go in the world.

I drop my bag off in my room and head down to the desk to give them my passport to put inside their safe since the room didn't have one. There's not a big time difference, so I'm not going to face jetlag, but I could use something to drink and maybe a bite to eat, so I head to the hotel's little restaurant.

I'm looking at the small paper menu they have at the table, trying to decide what to get to drink when the scent of Hermès d'Orange Verte creeps into my awareness.

I look up. Penelope. But out of context, it's like I almost don't recognize her for a moment, because why the hell would she be here of all places?

"Penelope?" I get up and hug her, enveloped in the older woman's scent. It's been a couple years, but she still feels like strength and safety. "What are you doing here?"

Penelope gives me a squeeze. "I'm here for you."

Tears of frustration well in my eyes. "Penny, someone did something to me. He released a video of me—of a JS party from years ago. I don't know how he got it."

She holds up her hand. "I know. And we're not about to let him get away with it."

Relief, gratitude, outrage, fear, disbelief war inside me for a moment. But underneath it all, affection for this woman. Old friend. Former lover.

See, when I'd said that Penelope had been the friend I'd so desperately needed, that was true. But we'd also been lovers. She lit up parts of me that I'd never felt before. I was her mistress. She made me feel so wanted and needed in a different way than a man, and I frantically needed that in my life then.

We parted ways in a remarkably drama-free manner, but she's still one of the people I think about the most fondly. Every split should go as well as ours did.

"How did you find me?" I ask.

"Does it matter?"

"No. You're right."

She tucks a lock of hair behind my ear and kisses my forehead. "Let's get your things and get out of here."

For the first time since the video was released—was it only a couple days ago?—I feel like things might be okay. I feel like I can relax because here is a woman who no one would dare mess with. Penelope is powerful, confident, and radiates competence. I am no longer alone in this battle.

Penelope and I take a car to the private jet she calls Winifred.

I don't ask where we're going. I trust this woman with my life. She already saved me once. I study her face when she's not looking, noting the new faint lines around her eyes and the way the ones around her mouth are a little deeper, though it hasn't been long since we last saw each other. What does a person like Penelope worry about?

About an hour later, the plane begins its descent and I peer out the window, suddenly curious about where we are.

A compound in the jungle. An exquisite community. We're flying low, low enough I can see details of the buildings and how they all flow perfectly together as one, some connected by indoor and outdoor bridges and meeting squares that extend into grand gardens, none of them private. Yet there's no one milling around outside, watering the lawn, and few cars are present. No kids are in sight.

We swoop lower, heading across the wall.

There's something written on the gate, ornate and in wrought-iron. I crane my neck and squint to see what the name of this place is. If it's pretentious or intellectual or raunchy—something to give me an idea of what it is before I land.

I recognize the words and a chill goes through me.

*I've seen those words before.*

An inscription is carved around its upper lip, and stained in red like a tattoo:

*Audācissimē Pēdite.*

*The ogre's mouth is open wide, as if it's laughing or screaming, I can't tell which...* And then again in a picture in my hand that wasn't a picture; it was a key. It was an answer that raised even more questions than before.

*I squint and zoom into the spot just above Inana's left shoulder. It's the view of a two-way mirror looking out—and it looks out into the VIP club below*

*La Notte—I recognize the bar from this angle even though the people in it are faded like ghosts and insubstantial.*

*I feel like if they were in the room beside Inana they'd still appear washed out next to her.*

*But the picture. The window. The mirror. It's a doorway, and now I know exactly where to go to find what comes next for myself.*

*I'd almost miss the words on the wall behind Inana.*

*Audācissimē Pēdite*

Those places were keys on the journey to whatever this place is. I've just flown past the door and am inside.

I've finally arrived.

I say the words aloud, likely butchering the pronunciation, but Penelope smiles.

"Yes. We are here."

I'm quaking inside, yet my hands are steady.

A driver picks us up and Penelope shows me to her house—a gorgeous Spanish-style villa. The ceilings are at least twenty feet high; the tiles gleam beneath my feet. There's lush carpeting that leads up the stairs to a second smaller great room and the master bedroom where the en suite is larger than my apartment.

Hell, the walk-in closet is larger than my apartment.

"Your home is lovely, Penelope."

Penelope laughs. "This isn't my home."

"Whose is it?"

"It's yours."

"Mine? What is this place?" I mean the island, not just the home.

"That is knowledge you must earn. But I will tell you that it belongs to The Juliette Society. Everyone here is a member. More importantly, it's safe for us and you'll have privacy."

I pick at my cuticles, trying to express my frustration while being granted…paradise. "I'm so grateful for the break, but my career has been taken and I want revenge on the bastard who's done it. I can't let him destroy my reputation and credibility." I can't bear to even say his name.

"More than a career is at stake here—and you can earn the life you want if you're willing to work for it. You've got a few days before the conference you came here for. I suggest using them to try this on. We're not letting the one who exploited you go unpunished, if that knowledge helps?"

I nod and relax a little. Penny always had a way of making me calmer, more settled. The conference isn't for a few days. A slow shiver rolls through my body. I'm on an island with only Juliette Society members.

Somehow I don't think they're here just to golf and lie on beaches.

I smile at Penelope and take a step closer to her.

# TWELVE

THE THING ABOUT PENELOPE IS that she has next to no body hair, almost as though she has neck-down alopecia. It can be a little unsettling at first, encountering no hair, not even peach fuzz, but after that initial surprise, you start thinking of ways to experience it.

My favorite was to make love to her in the shower, our bodies slipping over each other, my hands meandering over her impossibly smooth skin.

Those fine hairs you barely notice actually have a lot of texture and you don't realize that until they're gone. I also liked smoothing lotion onto her body, feeling it seep into her skin.

Penelope and I were always more about sensuality than fucking, taking our time undressing each other and laying kisses across the planes of each other's bodies.

She always smells so expensive and I don't know what exactly it is, but truly wealthy women have a certain scent, almost as though it's a pure, clean powder, but also perfume. It's not just their cosmetics, though they certainly add to it. Maybe it's more of an absence. The average person's clothes absorb the scents of life along their day, especially anything they cook. Elite people barely step foot inside a kitchen. It's rare to encounter one of them smelling of onions and garlic.

Penny smells clean but barely perfumed, as though that scent radiating from her is her unadorned skin. It's never offensive, but it makes you want to press your face against her and inhale deeply.

We're lying on our sides in bed, looking at each other. Naked, except for the crisp, cool sheets covering us from the waists down.

Penny's in great shape, but there's something about the way her skin stretches over her tiny collarbones that always makes me feel protective of her. This one delicate part of her body somehow makes me feel strong and vital in comparison.

She brushes my body softly with her hand in smooth, gentle strokes. I close my eyes and soak in the tenderness, letting her sweep away the tension of the last few days.

Her fingertips trace patterns over my skin, raising goosebumps all over my body. Her hands find my breasts and she massages them, lavishing care on them too, coaxing every last drop of pleasure she can from one erogenous zone before moving on to the next.

She likes to look you in the eyes when she makes you come.

It's not the hurricane of pleasure I felt with Dominick, but it's deep and strong, more like a whirlpool drawing you away from the shore and spinning you around and around in slow circles before pulling you under. Deep under until it's hard to breathe.

My hands join hers in a dance across her body, urging her breaths to come faster to match my own. Soon we're both wet and panting and writhing together.

I come first—Penny always found that a source of pride—and then lets me get her off when I've finished shaking with pleasure and release.

The best part of making love to a woman is that you don't have to wait for a cock to get hard before you can go again.

It's just orgasm after orgasm after orgasm until one of you—or both—passes out.

It's a great welcome to the island and a cap on the week.

I'm lying still when I wake up, not opening my eyes yet in case last night was a dream.

If I could choose a place to wake up from, if I could pick a point in my life to erase up until, I'm not sure where I'd choose. Erasing the leaked footage would be nice, but things would be the same unless I went back to that night and didn't participate.

And yet, that night was important, a catalyst. It also meant I lost Jack, but I know now that we were never destined to be together like I'd naively thought. I'd just have been fooling myself, dissatisfied for longer before the inevitable happened and we drifted further and further apart.

I could go back in time to before I'd met Jack, but I don't want to erase all of what we had together. If you take things back, you don't know what parts of yourself you have to return too, lessons won during the hard times that happened, the things you thought you'd never live through when your soul is lying in tatters on the floor.

Every experience makes us who we are. The good, the bad, and the ugly.

And somehow, I am in this place, this beautiful home that Penny says is mine and I'm trying to fathom what it all means. Have I arrived at a new place in my life, erasing everything else outside of it? Could I stay here forever and begin anew?

Could I let the things that happened in America be the ones that define who I was, and fade away from sight forever, wallowing in this community, whatever it is?

What is this place?

That's the thought that opens my eyes and I roll over to ask Penny. She is gone, but there's something on the pillow beside me, almost like a reward for getting where I'm supposed to be.

I sit up, fully awake.

I'd recognize that worn, dull red book anywhere.

I touch it, running my hands over the cover for a moment before flipping it open to see the familiar blue writing, slightly more faded than the last time I read the words.

*Hitting like a sharp, cold, punch of an early snowstorm. Skin's still inside the sunlight, remembering that warmth, and it feels every flake on itself like the edges are serrated.*

*Knives of pain that radiate. Radiation that turns inward, transforming into pleasure.*

*I am transformed.*

*And yet, the same.*

I flip more pages.

*How long can I go on? How far would I go? Eight's as good as seven. Twelve is as good as twenty. What's one more hour when you've gone for seventeen?*

*The orgasm is as devastating as the asteroid hurtling toward earth with our names on it—it's just a more pleasurable way to die.*

Inana Luna's diary in my hands again feels like coming home to a person I used to be.

*We're stuck deep inside, but the best way to feel connected to your body is to fuck someone else's. And yet, that act in itself, when done right, is the thing that frees us from our bodies, shows us our souls. Reminds us of our essences and we can once again see the face of gods.*

*There are more than we even fathom.*

*Sometimes gods walk around in human bodies, fooling us into thinking we're the apex of evolution when there's so much more staring us right in the face, watching, waiting.*

*Hungrily waiting for us to become more than what we are.*

*For them. For ourselves.*

I close the book, hugging it to my chest, overwhelmed at being reunited with Inana's personal thoughts and feelings. When the diary was taken from me I let it go, but never forgot the loss of it. How could you ever truly get over losing a part of yourself someone else found and wrote about? It was like finding myself.

But I accepted it when it was taken and replaced with the USB. Still, when I published Inana's story instead of reading the USB, it was like losing Inana. My memories of her words weren't good enough and all I had were the pages people had published online. A tiny fraction of the puzzle.

Had Penelope been the one to take the diary from me before?

I don't know. I don't think so, but in the end, it doesn't matter. I had to take the journey I'd taken to get here now, ready to embrace it. Did Inana ever make it here, or did her journey end at La Notte? Did she know about this place?

*We run from ourselves trying to find someone else. We embrace the darkness hoping for the light to shine on us and illuminate the truth when it's not that simple. It's not one or the other, it's one* and *the other.*

*Dualities.*

*Dualogies.*

*Dynamic duos.*

*Superheroes need a villain. They need the shadows to see the light. What is music without silence? Pain without pleasure. Black without white, water without wine, movies without movement.*

*Stasis is death.*

*Static is death.*

*Let go of intention and just be.*

Maybe things are predetermined. But I'm here now.

I'm here now. It doesn't matter what's happening on the news in America. It doesn't matter what people think. I'm far away for a moment and I will get the last word. Right now I need a break. So for a little while, I'm just going to be.

# THIRTEEN

BDSM HAS BECOME MORE AND more mainstream within the last few years as people aren't as histrionic and shockable as they once were. There's still that strange dichotomous taboo attached to sex that isn't there with violence. You can show someone's head being blown off, but more people are outraged when a woman breastfeeds in public.

We've become desensitized to violence. It makes sense that when attaching it to sex, it's still shocking. But kinks start out in the closet, and then come out into the mainstream, and just like every other fad, people want to try it. You don't want to be the last one to see that new blockbuster. You can't be the only one who hasn't read the "it" book of the day.

And that doesn't even broach clothing, shoes, and accessories. We are a nation of consumers, always looking toward the next hot ticket item, always saving for the next big thing that will drain us dry. See, people need goals to be happy. People need to be taught that they have to attain things, or society as we know it will collapse.

You hear people speak about a zombie apocalypse while munching on madeleines, but think if that actually happened.

The internet goes down, which means banks and commerce are done. Communication is gone except with people in your area. It wouldn't take long for the world to implode into anarchy, but that wouldn't last forever. It behooves people to be moral. If the majority of people were running around killing each other, civilization wouldn't work. Deviant behavior is deviant from the norm. And most people are innately good and don't want to hurt each other.

But some people do.

And some people want to be hurt.

I read once about a couple of men who found each other in an online ad. One put the ad up, saying he wished to be tortured and killed. The man who answered the ad wanted to torture and kill someone.

It seems like a match made in heaven until you take the laws into account. It was argued that the man who wrote the ad was mentally disturbed and not in his right mind, and the other took advantage of the situation. He went to jail despite the victim leaving behind a detailed letter absolving the other of any responsibility.

But was he truly a victim? We'll never know what happened, if at the end he had regrets but was too far gone—or the man who killed him was too far gone and didn't listen when told to stop.

I'm pretty sure cannibalism was involved.

Sometimes from the outside, something seems strange and harmful when really it's exactly what people are looking for.

This is especially true when it comes to sex. We've all heard about something that raised our eyebrows. Infantilism, pony play. Furries. Sure, the first time you hear about anything new when it comes to sex can be strange, laughable even. There was a heavyset man who made headlines for preferring the holes of Swiss cheese over a woman's. I think about that often. I wonder if the fetish was more texture or scent based. I'd have to imagine scent maybe it brought him to a special place in his memory.

I mean, do you remember the first time you hear about being eaten out? "You want to lick me where? Why? That's gross!" Then when you were older it happened and goddamn, suddenly you understood completely why people would do that.

Even kissing sounds strange when you break it down. "I'm going to put my lips against yours, and we're going to move our heads around. Tongues will touch and rub together and maybe nibbling will happen. No, it feels good, trust me."

Sometimes describing the mechanics falls woefully short of the acts themselves.

But back to BDSM.

There are a lot more toys and tools than you'd think, and varieties of each. Even your favorite online store sells sex toys now. People used to have to go inside seedy little shops to get tools to help them get their freak on, and look people in the eye while buying a vibrating, two-headed, spiked dildo.

Some people are embarrassed to step foot inside a sex shop, which I find as ridiculous as the people who are too embarrassed to buy tampons or toilet paper at stores. They're tools we all use. Who's to say you're not going to take that cucumber or carrot and cram it in your ass later on a quiet Tuesday night? Facts are facts. We all shit, and we all masturbate. If you're going to masturbate, you might as well use a tool that makes it the best experience it can be.

If you're going to fuck, you might as well try to give your partner the best experience of their life. BDSM is the same.

Penelope finds me still reading the diary, and gently smiles and tells me she wants to show me something. I follow her to a room down the hall that's larger than I expected with hunter green walls and light hardwood floors. There are cabinets on the walls with no doors, but it isn't until Penny flips a second switch on the wall that the cabinets light up as well and reveal their contents.

Whips, chains, restraints, crops, lubes, dildos, vibrators.

It's a kinkster's wet dream. Possibly literally.

I do a slow perimeter walk around the room, gazing into all the cabinets as Penelope talks.

"These are all yours, to do with as you wish. You can choose not to use any of them, simply keeping it body to body with no toys. But you must learn how to use all of them. Some I know we're both familiar with, but now you must master them all to please your lovers—if you want any. You know what we are, Catherine. Hopefully, you're learning who you are too."

I nod.

She smiles and rubs her hands together. "Let's start with one of our favorites…butt plugs?" She poses it as a question instead of an order, a great way to get me comfortable.

I understand people's aversion to anal play. Anything where poop is involved isn't innately sexy—unless you're into that, which I'm not. Guys seem to have a fascination with it right off the bat which seems strange, but I saw a guy fucking a tailpipe in a car in a video on the internet the other day, so not much shocks me anymore when it comes to the things guys want to stick their dicks into.

I've never gotten why they don't teach more about exploration and pleasuring yourself in sex education in school. My experience may be different from yours, but it was very much a vanilla, heterosexual, normative narrative with very little deviation from the missionary script. Why do we teach teenagers all about wars and quadratic equations, but not let them know that it's okay to explore their own bodies? I understand not wanting to encourage sex when they're young, but masturbation?

If you want to be scared, use a blacklight in a teenage boy's bedroom. I'm pretty sure you could see that shit from space if you did it at night. Besides, if people were regularly—and effectively— getting themselves off, they'd know how to get each other off when they're ready to have sex.

But even within the "safe" topics in school, they never talked about anal sex, or gay sex at all. Hardly anything for oral as well, which is a shame. If they're trying to educate teenagers, they should be educating them about everything without excluding non-heterosexual norms. I mean, what message is that sending to LGBT kids?

That they're different.

That their sex doesn't count.

It's not fair or right.

And they can say it's a percentage thing all they want—that only a small portion of the population is LGBT, so they simply don't have the time to get into specifics of all kinds. But straight people like having anal sex, too.

I wonder if that was originally on the agenda for sex education classes, and then someone's sanctimonious wife who thinks sex outside of missionary is degrading to women decided that anal was off limits to talk about. Because this is all run by men. And do you know the percentage of men who want to try anal?

If someone said your chances of winning the lottery were that high, you'd buy a ticket.

Instead, we're taught that anal is something, within straight couples, that a woman does for the man on special occasions—or, if she thinks his eye is wandering and she wants to spice things up a little. Something that she can't enjoy because it's going to be painful and terrible. Women are taught to fear anal, that it's going to be uncomfortable and awful and to get it over with quickly if you do it at all.

Maybe some people won't ever like it. A lot of us do. But people are missing out on it because of the programming we're incorrectly taught. If you haven't tried it before, go now. Get acquainted with your asshole. Stop thinking of it as exit only and see if you like how it feels when you play with it a little. Or a lot.

Use lube.

This goes for men, too.

There are a few of those butt plugs with long, swishy faux fur tails attached, for if someone wants to take being a sexy kitty to the next level on Halloween—or whenever. I saw an article online once where a mom had gotten one of those "tails" for her daughter's Halloween costume from Etsy, but didn't understand how she was supposed to attach it.

Of course, people lost their minds at her cluelessness.

To be fair, I don't find them that sexy either, but it's mostly because they're just kind of...limp. If one stuck up like a squirrel's that could be cute, but the way most of them are it looks like you're taking a dump and passing a fuzzy turd that hasn't fallen yet.

I pass a cabinet with a few different strap-ons, which makes me think of pegging. Strap-ons aren't only for lesbians to use on each other. See, the male G-spot, a.k.a. the prostate, is inside their asses. It's like God was saying, maybe you need to take it once in a while too, if you want the really deep orgasm. You're never going to know what makes you come the hardest unless you commit to a lot of effort and experimentation.

There's nothing against the law about that.

Speaking of the law, I pass a restraints section filled with all kinds of methods and materials for tying someone up or strapping someone down. Leather D-ring cuffs always bring to mind insane asylums and the things I shouldn't think are kinky—being a patient there and getting restrained and fucked by a sexy nurse—but I do.

What can I say, sometimes we just really like some problematic shit.

In among the fancier cuffs are a few pairs of good, old fashioned steel handcuffs like the ones police carry. I wonder which came first—handcuffs as restraints or the sexy cop fantasy. Did some kinky fuck get picked up by a police officer and unleash a subgenre of fantasies as soon as the cold metal closed around their wrists?

Were handcuffs always sexy, or did they become that way when strapped to a big, strong cop with chiseled features and a cool exterior you were itching to crack?

It's funny how an instrument can be sexy or terrifying depending on the context. Handcuffs, blindfolds...duct tape. Everyone's mileage varies as well. Some people love adrenaline rushes and perceived danger more than others.

It's the same with pain. Sexual masochists are into pain, get off on it, but I can't see how something sexy like getting thrashed by a Dominant compares to the pain of someone accidentally stepping on your toe, or getting a tooth drilled at the dentist and the anesthetic wearing off a couple minutes too early. But it's about choice.

When we want to hone our pleasure with pain, when we want to achieve that perfect balance of the senses, it's about knowing what we're getting into beforehand.

Do I want someone to use a cane on me while ramming a vibrator in my pussy?

Do I want to be tied up and suspended and tased on a low setting while someone eats my pussy?

Do I want to be fucked to the point of orgasm and have someone choke me until I almost pass out, only letting me breathe right as I come?

It doesn't matter if a concept is gross to you. Someone else may love it.

I had sex with a guy for the first time a couple years ago, and gasped because when he took off his shirt, there was a giant eye of Sauron tattooed on his chest. It was very distracting to look up because my eye level was at his chest, so the tattoo was just staring me in the face the whole time, like being fucked by the All-Seeing Eye. It didn't help that he was as tall as an average basketball player, so my eyes couldn't look away from it.

Maybe someone else would have wanted to shove a ring in his hole, but the tattoo didn't do it for me. I'm just saying, there's something out there for everyone.

My playroom is amazing and I can't wait to explore every inch of it like a new lover.

I was born to be in this place.

# FOURTEEN

I'M LYING IN THE BATHTUB, soaking away the fluids of the day, flipping through Inana's diary. Inside the back cover, someone has tucked a few pages that were torn out at the end. She's drawn a few exotic flowers I recognize as being native to the compound.

*When I am all that's left, I'll be half of what I'll be, but twice the woman I was. Shedding illusion and other people's perception like a snake is the key to breathing deeply.*

*Air is life. Life is an illusion. Lies are an illusion.*

*Where illusions die, real life explodes into conscious color, revealing the trappings in the shadows you never knew were there.*

*He'll be there.*

*We'll be there.*

*The further I go in this journey, the farther I want to go.*

*I wonder where I'll be…someday.*

I'm wondering what things Inana would have done if she'd lived. Would she have moved on to another form of expression? Unless she'd become one of those artists who cut themselves and literally make art from their blood on a canvas, she didn't have much room to take things further.

There's always a pinnacle when it comes to art until it gets ridiculous or becomes a caricature of itself.

A raw meat dress.

Showing up to an exhibition in a limousine full of turnips.

There's something to be said for shock value. It wakes us up and gets our attention. It's a creative slap in the face that can startle us out of our comfy ruts. It makes a statement that things are shitty, or getting shitty, and need to change now.

But there's a line between a statement and a mockery. Sometimes people try to provoke a reaction, they'll go as far as they can until people say something. Others eventually get so fed up they'll do anything to try to get you to see how ridiculous their product is. Depending on who you are, people may never say anything, instead applauding louder and louder until you can't think and even you buy into your own lies because you can no longer hear the truth.

It's like the old story about the Emperor and his new clothes. It was ridiculous, but he wasn't called out for a ridiculously long time because no one wanted to be the one who couldn't see the value in the illusion. They couldn't pretend to see it so they'd continue to fit in. It's amazing how scared people are of going against the grain, of standing out, when so many want to be famous or celebrities.

Dolly the sheep, ready for her close up, Mr. DeMille.

People don't want to see what they've already seen, what's already been done unless they're looking for a train wreck that's going to be entertaining as hell. That's why people were so eager to share the news about my video. I'm visible enough for people to sort of know who I am, more importantly they now perceive me as being some sort of celebrity and enjoying privileges they likely don't. There's the perception that I can be torn down from an ivory tower, as it were.

If you heard that an acquaintance had been filmed during sex without her permission and the tape was released, you'd likely be horrified and outraged, putting yourself in her position, thinking how you'd feel.

But when it's a celebrity, you become ravenous. You want to see the videotape, see what she looks like naked, see if her body is as perfect as it is when it's been airbrushed or if there's secretly bands of cellulite beneath her ass, or stretch marks on her hips. If it's a guy, you want to see how big his cock is, if it goes left or right, is he cut or uncut. Does his cock "justify" his cockiness.

You want the flaws. You feel entitled to them as if they were your own and you'd paid for them. You want to see if there's a scar to prove she had implants. You don't feel bad because celebrities have no privacy—they waived that right by putting themselves out there.

Having your life and every moment of it scrutinized and your character and image ripped to shreds every moment of every day is a small price to pay for the lifestyle they have.

Or so you think. I don't even enjoy that lifestyle, as I'm just a reporter and work my ass off, but because people think I must surely get to since I interview some of the people who live behind the velvet rope.

They'd be shocked at some of the celebrities and what they're really like behind closed doors. Paranoid, insecure, petty. Down to earth, friendly, genteel.

They're all different. Some are true narcissists. You have to be if you're in any kind of art or field where you're creating a product for others to consume. Otherwise you'd never think people wanted what you were selling and you'd never bother trying to create it. Others only know how to live as another character. Sometimes we trap others with our perception of them, with the expectation of what we see.

People in uniforms, for example, have a way of becoming fetishes. The sexy cop, the sexy firefighter. They become the service they provide. Wink.

But there's one profession I've been thinking about more recently, getting off to, even fucking a few of them.

Servers. Specifically waitresses. There's a familiarity with them, a sort of interchangeability because of their uniforms: white top, black skirt or pants—I find the pants sexier than skirts, personally. More utilitarian and unconsciously sexy than a skirt with heels. Despite the fact they're all unique human beings with a whole life behind them, most of the time they're unseen by those they strive to serve, fading into the background by choice or design.

Their whole purpose is to make your experience smooth and enjoyable and they take so much bullshit from those people a lot of the time. Rude behavior, outright abuse, condescension, shitty tippers, the list goes on. But they're there with a smile and a refill and if you're a) not rude to them, and b) attracted to them, there's a connection that can happen with them.

The anonymity of it all is a turn on. You get to create a narrative about who they truly are behind the uniform and script they're forced to say.

Is the lady bringing the ketchup also a dancer, and beneath the clothes she's got an ass you could bounce quarters off of, and those unfortunately ugly ballerina feet?

Is the woman filling your glass doing this to save up for college where she's studying particle physics and that's why she didn't need to write a word of your table's complicated orders down?

Virgin, insatiable sex fiend, sparkly wit, or studious nature, we get to choose what we see. We get to create their background and place that inside their uniforms along with their bodies. The uniforms make everyone equally mysterious and sexy. They're an equalizer. It's fun to take one of them home and make them scream your name, and then discover if the story you made up for them matches the reality at all.

It always comes back to fantasy vs reality. Even with Hollywood and celebrities, they cultivate their brands and feed your expectations.

Inana knew her brand, knew her market and eschewed expectations, which should have made things harder or put her at risk of

alienating her fans, but it didn't. When you don't care about alienating people, you gain the freedom to do the things you want to do—
and you're the reason they started following. Not everyone will like
everything you do, but stay true to your vision and you'll gain new
followers to replace ones who part ways with your journey.

But the places Inana could have gone...I bet they'd have been
outstanding. The places Anna could have gone would have been
outstanding. I'd have liked to have seen her and Inana together.

I wonder if she'd have liked me. Would we have clicked when
we met, if we'd met at a TJS party? I think she'd met Anna, but I
don't know if they hung out. I can't imagine people inside the society
doing something casual outside of it. The experiences are too intense
for that. When you've caught a glimpse of the fire in someone else's
belly, it's hard to dim it down, fade it, to talking about the mundane
over a coffee.

But what about if we'd met at a party, at an event put on by and
for The Juliette Society? We'd recognized in each other the spark of
willingness and daring, but I'm stronger in myself now than I was
with Anna as my sort of leader in those experiences. What if that
happened now?

What would that be like?

I picture those eyes of hers, piercing and flirty, making contact
with mine across the room. Her lips would stretch into a smile
mirroring my own, and I'd be drawn towards her as she was drawn
to me, each recognizing in the other that we are the same.

I cup my breasts and play with my nipples a little, pinching the
tips until they're darker and tingling.

Anna would move in that sinuously graceful way she had, like
a cat on the prowl even though she was most content on her knees
instead of being the hunter. She flowed. I'd snap and flicker, the fire
to her water, energetic and mesmerizing because I'd rise to the occasion to be as beautiful as her.

Maybe I'm already as beautiful as her.

My hands skim down my belly to my pubic mound, and I knead it, not allowing myself to touch my clit yet.

In my vision of Anna and I there's actual fire and water, waves of heat and coolness rippling and dancing along with us as we weave around each other, naked in the darkness now, twisting around each other in a complicated dance we both somehow know the steps to. I splash warm water over my crotch, feeling it trickle between the lips of my pussy, adding heat to my skin, increasing circulation, making me throb before I inch my hand closer to my clit.

The light glimmers off our glistening bodies and there's a wall of bodies all around us, watching and waiting to see what we'll do next, people in black bottoms and white tops. There's an electricity in the air that almost crackles to the beat of the music that seems to originate with our feet stomping on the floor.

I slide one wet finger, then another, inside myself, letting the warmth flood me from within, pulling at my hole so the water enters me, and I slosh it around with my fingers, mixing it with my come.

Smiling at her, I trace my collarbones and nape of my neck, feeling the weight of my hair as I pull my fingers through it and let it drop down, the ends tickling my back. Anna does a spin, her hair whirling out, sending ripples of blue in an arc, splashing against the skin of the spectators.

My fingers punish my pussy, slamming in and out, working my G-spot and my clit at once, and I stretch my legs up and rest them on the wall.

The energy we create together with our dancing, simply by being in the same place at the same time together again, is electric.

Anna's lips part. "Come, Catherine. Show them all."

Her words wind around my throat and down between my breasts, sliding between my legs, making me come in concentric waves of pleasure that crash over me again and again and again.

The image breaks apart, morphing into the sage green walls of my bathroom.

A tear slips down my cheek as I pull my fingers out from my pussy. We could have been amazing together.

But now I'll never know what that might have been like. When someone dies before their time, we lose their potential as well. And we will never know what connections we could have made that may have led to another, enriching our lives in untold ways.

I get out of the tub and slather lotion on my skin, inhaling the delicate freesia scent.

I once went on a double date with a co-worker. Neither she nor I went on another date with either of those guys, but a few months later I ran into them. They'd become roommates, strictly platonic, even though they'd never met before the night we'd all gone out.

You never know which connections you'll forge for other people or through them. Anna and I may have grown apart after the honeymoon period wore off, and gone our separate ways. We may have become best friends who lasted until our bones crumbled. We could have been catalysts for other people in ways that rippled out, changing the world in myriad ways.

But she was taken from the world—and she's not the only one.

I mourn the loss of the women like Inana and Anna and myself men take out along the way because they can't possess us and it's the worst thing in the world to them. Instead of choosing another partner, they destroy us.

I can't let Dominick win. I'm tired of the man being the one standing at the end in a position of power, laughing over the ruination of a young, sweet, thing.

I don't know what his motivation is, why he would try to discredit me or ruin my life this way simply for turning him down. All I know is I won't let it happen. There's more to me now than that girl in the chair on the video that night. More grit, more resolve, more steel in her spine. She was all submissive, no dominant. Not even a switch although the switch inside her was there, waiting, watching, hungry for both.

There are a lot of us who like both. Who like it all. Sometimes to see how much you can take, and sometimes to see how much you can get. Some are just voracious for a taste of everything on their tongues and when the experience is gone they need more to replace it.

I'm thinking about what Inana's journey was, and the way she dominated and submitted. I don't think she had a true preference. But it's like Janus. Looking forward and back. Being on top looking down, and on the bottom looking up—assuming it's missionary position, of course.

We've got to choose to look back at the past and miss out on the things coming our way, or face the new things in life head on. We can't do both at the same time. We have to pick up the severed pieces of our past and become new again.

# FIFTEEN

PENNY TOLD ME TO DRESS for dancing, and is leading me
to a corner of the compound. The buildings are larger like a classic
French chalet, and farther apart. I realize the paths and each home
like mine are connected. I hear music but the grand door we stop in
front of gives me no indication of what might lie behind it; it seems to
show age though I know this place has to be new. Beige metal siding,
brownish roof, flat top. The windows have coverings on them and no
light escapes them to give me a hint of tonight's activity.

We walk into a large room which resembles the inside of a ware-
house, but it's not empty. Instead, there's a club inside, pulsing with
sound and heat and people. I can hear them but they're still out of
sight behind two large closed doors.

"Welcome, Catherine, to the island," Penny says with a pleased
smile.

"Did you make me a party?" I ask.

"Of course." She shouldn't have, but that's Penelope's style.

There's a quote on the door, and she waits until I read it and
smile. "Rabelais," I identify it. It's a quote from Rabelais' bawdy epic

*Gargantua and Pantagruel*, a story I fell in love with while over in Paris with Penelope.

She inclines her head. "Precisely."

It's a story we used to discuss at length. Some people bond over a song, or a film. We bonded over the epic tale, and would discuss it at length over wine and cheese and bread, as it was meant to be, like everything French.

The language used was interesting, Rabelais actually inventing some of the words, much like Shakespeare used to do. *Gargantua and Pantagruel* is no Shakespeare, but it's a fairly irreverent journey through decadence and scathing social commentary, especially about the Catholic Church and Catholicism. While that may not sound like much of anything now, at the time it was risqué, and stirred up quite the controversy, even couched in the ridiculous as it was.

It was different from anything I'd ever read before, and I was delighted by the whole tale, particularly the section about the Abbey of Theleme, a utopian society dreamed up by Rabelais that organized itself under the motto "Do What Thou Wilt" and inspired a real-life secret sex society, the Hellfire Club, which Benjamin Franklin was said to be a member of during the time he lived in England. Other clubs have tried to take its place, one rather blatantly using the motto *uno avulso non defecit alter*—when one is torn away another succeeds. But there's great deviation from the exploits of the modern clubs and those of the predecessors.

Penelope swings the doors open, and the music changes from techno to pumped up classical on steroids, more like electric violins and harpsichords, as smoke billows out of the darkness. I recognize parts of the story in the décor of the room.

We walk inside the doors, past large white stalactites and stalagmites, and it takes me a second to realize they're supposed to be Pantagruel's teeth. We all enter the club like the natives who lived inside his mouth. There's a world inside a mouth. We're inside his mouth. No wonder it's hot and muggy.

The men and women are all dressed as characters from the story. Lots of loincloths, likely because of the ease of removal, judging by the amount of oral sex that's already happening in dark corners of the room.

There are beds made up of large models of body parts, like a giant in repose, for those who wish to use them. A giant's foot houses a king sized bed on the top, a bent man embraces the big toe while another man takes him from behind as the first licks between a woman's toes, worshipping them with his tongue as she reclines on the bed eating grapes. For someone with a foot fetish, that would be heaven.

There's part of a massive ship, sawn in half and attached to the wall like it's sailing into the horizon. The sea monster they slay is even there, lurking in the water around the ship's hull. The wall around it has been painted with an elaborate sunset to further enhance the fantasy. It must have taken days to create and execute, but there's no scent of fresh paint, only pleasing herbs and a gentle perfume of flowers and salt to enhance the illusion of being at sea as if we were Fellini's audience. Men dressed as pirates fuck women and men dressed as mermaids, complete with tails, writhing around in the water, making the water splash over the sides of the area it's contained in onto the sand where two grown men make sandcastles together as though they're children.

I always wondered if people who thought mermaids were hot had fish fetishes. Because if you look, mermaids have nothing to fuck. There'd be a cold, slimy hole at best, and nothing on the men—unless their penises would go from innies to outies, but if that's the case, they're probably more like a button than a nice, big cock. Sure the girls have nice, long hair and good tits, but I don't know about the fin situation. To each his own, I guess.

Penelope's even included the women so fat they cut into their own skin to let the fat out, only they're wearing suits filled with liquor and people get to stab the suit and suckle as much as they want from them. Penny offers me a short knife, and I head to one of the women, sliding the tip of the blade in before letting the slowly oozing liquid coat my tongue. It's sweet and spicy and thicker than I expected, more like spiced liquid honey than wine, but it's delicious and I suck and lick at it until the place I stabbed dries up.

I stand and thank the woman, but her eyes are closed and her lips move as though in prayer or meditation.

A sign above the bar says, Trincs, to mirror the fifth book, which I'm not sure was actually written by Rabelais himself, or cobbled together from bits of first draft ideas and smoothing from the publisher, or if it was truly original material. There were some solid ideas in there, nonetheless. But it's like the more controversial speeches by Hecate in Shakespeare's *Macbeth*. Some of the language is different enough that there are some who say it had to have been penned by someone else and sandwiched in.

I ask Penelope about this. She shrugs. "Regardless of whether or not the parts were written by the author or someone else, they're part of the story now."

I agree. And yet, if I was able to get my hands on a time machine, I'd go back to Shakespeare's time to see if he was a singular man, or a shared pen name many of the most successful writers of the era used.

He was certainly prolific enough for me to buy that theory. It almost beggars belief to think of all the amazing things he wrote in one lifetime—and that's not even including the pieces he wrote and discarded, or all the time it took to polish his plays and sonnets into the way we know them today. One person undertaking all of that in one lifetime seems impossible.

But I'd rather he was one amazing person who gave us all those beautiful works. I love the idea of one person being that important to the world, even if they're not around to see it happen. Maybe it's better if you don't know how important you are to the world, only that people in it loved and cared about you, because if you knew everything you did was going to be recorded, you'd start being more careful, taking fewer risks.

Penelope parades me through the center of the room, up a path inlaid with words written in what appears to be Latin, but I can't quite see in the dim lighting and we're moving too fast for me to stop and check.

Besides, there are more interesting things happening here than what some words on the flood say. I can always ask Penny later if I want.

Everyone smiles at me as I pass, but the party doesn't stop because I've walked in, which I prefer. If everyone's watching my every move, it's not going to be possible to fully relax and enjoy myself without feeling like I'm performing. It's a party for me, not about me, and that's the key difference that dulls the self-consciousness a few notches, which is good when things suddenly flip and men and women lie on the floor in front of me, exposing their backs.

I don't question it. I simply walk across them, trying not to let my heels dig in too badly, but not tiptoeing either. I mean, they did this for a reason. Everyone else crowds closer, standing at the heads and feet of the people on the floor, literally building a fleshy corridor with their bodies for me to head down. People moan when I step on them, and more than a few backs crack.

I wonder if this is how chiropractors started.

But walking on top of them, feeling their skin slip around on top of their bones, makes me feel powerful. It makes me feel revered.

My corridor ends with a throne of sorts. Red velvet cushions the oversized dark wooden chair, chocolate in color. It takes me a moment to realize the engraving at the top is the letter C.

C for Catherine?

My throne.

I practically run across the last bodies and head up the shiny black steps and touch the seat of power with trembling fingertips.

I'm not sure what's making me so emotional in this moment, only that it feels like I've been waiting for it for too long and my brain can't process that this is all real.

I'm not the prettiest, or the smartest, or most successful in the room. I'm not the wealthiest, or most talented. But they're all going out of their way to elevate me. They're all letting me into their fantasies, stripping away everything except our desires. They're putting on a show for me.

A man crawls up to me, taking his position like he's my ottoman and I asked to put my feet up, though my lips have never parted.

As though we do this every day.

He shudders when I move him into a slightly better position using only my feet.

The people who let me walk on them now stand, and reveal a chessboard on the floor. Penelope stands on a dais above one side, a woman I've never met on the other.

They put on a chess match, acting out the moves with their bodies and large painted squares on the floor, like they're the part of the Queendom of Whims.

If they are, that makes me the queen, I suppose, seeing as how I'm the one on the throne, being entertained. I should feel awkward about the fuss being made, but I don't.

The losing pieces of the chess match are made to sit on the sidelines on benches with the seats cut out while other party guests come up behind them and slick whichever hole they want with lube, and stick whatever they want into those holes, not that the guests mind.

Fingers, toes, cocks, I even see a banana employed into a man's asshole while he arches along with the bend in the fruit as it disappears into his ass.

It's hot to watch people who love getting used get what they want.

Someone rings a bell, and everyone pauses as people walk onto the chessboard and place vibrators inside the remaining pawns on both sides, fixing them in place before tying the pawns' hands behind their necks so they can't touch the vibrators to remove them or use them.

The game continues, Penny and her opponent calling out moves and the players following their instructions. Eyes roll back into heads and hips buck, thighs clench, trying to get relief from the stimulation, but they're not allowed to move from their places.

It makes the game a little more interesting when people fall to their knees with tears dripping down their faces. Semen spurts out onto the floor. Moans fill the air. Still, the game continues. One of the Bishops from the white side starts fucking a pawn in the ass and she smiles back at him, so grateful for his cock.

Happy all the way to the floor as they tumble down, rutting and fucking, barely noticing as they're herded off the board and their team loses two pieces just like that.

Penelope's winning.

I tap my ottoman with my toe. "What's your name?"

"Whatever you want it to be, Mistress."

I spread my legs and gesture him closer.

And like the good piece of furniture he is, he shuts up and does his job, pushing up my skirt, moving my panties to the side, and burying his face between my legs, eating me out with an enthusiasm that would be embarrassing if it wasn't making me wet as hell. He licks and sucks at me while I watch other people lick and suck at each other, getting off at my party.

Being here is like crawling inside a well-loved story and living inside it for a while. Everything is warm and comforting, even though some things should be startling or scary. They're familiar like old friends. It's perfect as a welcome party because it's like coming home.

And there's nothing more welcoming than that.

Well, except for the tongue between my legs.

# SIXTEEN

CLUBS ON THE ISLAND ARE pretty much the same as in America.

Except that here, you can trust everyone because they've been vetted, and they're more about sex than music.

Here, you don't face the disappointment of expectations not being met by reality when you take someone home, hoping they're into the same things you are.

Sure, they may not be into all of the same things either, but it's not because they're going to judge you for wanting something they don't. It just might mean you've picked up a submissive instead of a dominant. There's less of a danger here and more of a thrill.

Or maybe that's my way of letting my guard down because tonight I want to be thoroughly fucked.

The man staring at me from across the bar won't leave my gaze. His hair is a little long, but he's clean-shaven, the smoothness revealing the strong lines of his jaw and the slight dimple in his chin. Beards have become trendy in the last couple of years, but I've seen quite a few "with" versus "without" shots of guys with beards, and while I tend to prefer a clean-shaven guy, beards truly can hide a multitude of sins.

This guy doesn't seem to have any.

He sips his scotch, neat, and the bevels in the crystal glass kick back an amber refraction against the dark bar from the overhead lights. I make a little show of sipping my vodka soda slowly, letting the tip of my tongue linger on the tip of the straw, letting him get my hint.

He watches for a moment, head slightly bowed, before standing and moving to stand in front of me. His dark eyes remind me of the perfect sensation of bittersweet chocolate melting on my tongue, and when he offers his hand, I accept it. I want to taste the places he's going to take me. Instead of leading me, he actually picks me up, carrying my body like I'm a damsel in distress. I laugh inside.

Down a hallway with sloping arches and dark purple walls, I let him carry me away, as though floating inside a current, past other doorways hung with brightly hued floating fabric. We get to a room at the back, separated from the rest with a gauzy orange curtain. Purple and gold wallpaper done in a Moroccan-style pattern adorns the walls of the small, round room.

It's warm inside and almost muggy. Or maybe it only feels that way because I expect to be awash with a jasmine-scented fog as soon as the fabric swishes to cover the door behind us, giving us privacy but not security, which makes me think someone's waiting to watch us—or already here watching. The thought isn't offensive, though it's something I've done before and doesn't give me the buzz of novelty.

About a year ago now, I was dating a voyeur, and picked up a couple guys at a strip club to bone. He was hiding in the closet and I was trying to get them both to fuck me at once but they were chicken, and both acting like they were so macho that seeing each other naked wasn't within the realm of possibility. That just meant they'd already fooled around after having a few beers, but whatever. The guy I was dating was still hiding in the closet. I was going to take the friends one at a time in the bedroom—and by one at a time I mean they wouldn't even bone me with each other in the same room, like it was going to make them gay or something. I fucked one guy, then he left, and his friend came in. But before we fucked, I left the room. To grab a drink? To pee? I forget. But as I was coming back, the second guy went to the living room and was frantically telling the first guy that there was someone in the closet. And the first guy was like, "What are you talking about? There is no guy in the closet."

I managed to convince the first dude that the second one was just super wasted and not making sense so he should take his friend home. The second guy was giving me daggers the whole time, but was also too freaked out to say more.

In that case it wasn't hot, because the one guy ruined it. You'd think he'd have realized it was a bit of harmless fun when nothing bad happened to his friend who went first. It was a bust but not the first—or last—time I did something like that for the guy I was dating. I always wondered if Marcus might have done something similar with Anna.

This guy sets me on my feet but keeps me close, hauled right up against him to feel his hard cock against my hip. I rub him through his pants, knowing the fabric takes the edge off the pleasure, making it duller, making it less satisfying, making him want more.

I want to take it slow to give anyone watching a better show. I reach down the front of his pants, circling his girthy cock between my fingers and giving it a little clench as the fabric around it doesn't allow me enough room to stroke it like I want to, the way he'd like.

He's warm and smooth and his hands squeeze my ass and he bends slightly to kiss me, but before our lips meet, someone behind me clears their throat in that annoying "hem hem" way people do when they're obviously trying to get your attention without actually using their words.

I turn to look at the interrupter. He's good looking, in his late fifties or early sixties, and obviously takes care of himself. He's got the physique of someone who used to lift a lot of weights, or participate in a sport on a professional level, but gave it all up to get into business and now only plays on the weekends and takes it a little too seriously.

Something in the frown lines between his eyes supports that, like he could never have a friendly game of racketball or golf. He'd be working out the angles instead of trying to bond with you while on the course. The way he looks at me sends a spiral up my spine.

Not quite fear, but an alert awareness that tells every instinct in my body, every single nerve ending to quiver and be ready because things could get seriously bad in a hurry.

He's Mr. X. I know it.

"Catherine. What do you think of the place?" He spreads his hands proudly, heavily implying it's all his or that he's a major player. Maybe he means the compound, maybe just the club, I don't know.

But he acts oblivious to the fact that I've got another guy's cock in my hand, and that's strange. I also notice he doesn't ask how I got here, or seem at all surprised to find me in one of the back rooms at his club and he should, unless he's been watching me. Of course he has been.

I release the stranger's dick and surreptitiously wipe my hand on the cushion next to me. "I ran into Penelope at my hotel on the mainland. She invited me here. Can't say that it's been a terrible imposition, but..." I grin, going for humor about the situation.

He raises his eyebrows. "I didn't know you and Penelope are friends."

He seems put out. Have I screwed up? But why would he care? Do he and Penelope have issues, or is it that he had wanted to be the one initiating me into this, bringing me to the compound himself? I've never gotten a sexual vibe off him, so it can't be jealousy, can it?

Mr. X jerks his head toward the door and the guy I came with walks out of the room, leaving Mr. X and me all alone.

"I'm glad you're fitting in so well among our members, but this place isn't without...dangers."

I frown. "I'm not sure what you mean. Everyone's been so nice." I'll play dumb and see where this goes.

"There's a reason I brought you down here to cover the conference. You may hear," he waves his hands as though thinking about his words, "some things."

"What kind of things?" I ask, my curiosity rearing up and taking notice. Finally, we get to his real agenda.

His eyes get a flat, dead look to them and he steps into my space. "It doesn't matter. I brought you here to write the story I want you to write."

"And if I don't?"

His smile shows perfect teeth but doesn't reach his eyes. "This is my world. And in my world, people who cause trouble have a funny little habit of going missing. Women who give me grief have this thing in common where they disappear and are either found later... or not at all. You don't want to be one of the women whose stories you tell, Catherine."

Is he saying he killed Inana? That he killed Anna as well? The bastard smiles as though we've just shared a laugh. His eyes fucking twinkle with mirth. I've known men who were bastards and men who were powerful. But I've never before spoken to someone who I believe could whistle over my corpse as he stepped over it and moved on to his next victim.

My body breaks out in goosebumps when he taps beneath my chin in an almost grandfatherly gesture before walking out of the room, leaving me alone with his threats and too many questions.

I don't think he's bluffing, but I wonder if he was the guy Anna was seeing and if he's the reason Anna went missing as well. But vague threats don't necessarily mean real danger, and I highly doubt Anna ever would have tried to expose anyone for kink when she was neck deep in it herself.

I stand rigidly, still not sure if I'm being watched or filmed, as my mind races as fast as my pulse. After a few deep breaths rationality gradually comes back into the picture. He's not going to kill me. I've got powerful friends of my own. I'm in a safe place. I've earned my place here.

So what is it about Mr. X? What does he get out of relationships with people? I'm trying to wrap my head around this guy. Why he is so absent and mysterious, but wanting to be involved, though not romantically, with me and my career. He seems annoyed not that I'm here, but that Penny—or anyone other than himself—brought me here. Does he want me to feel like I owe him?

Having someone in your debt means you've got a certain amount of control over them. There's an imbalance there that needs to be settled at some point. That must be it. The only thing I can deduce is that he has a fetish for power. He thinks I'm his toy, his prize pawn. He enjoys feeling as though he's "made me" in some way. Maybe he'd provided the opportunity, but I'd done the work myself and he couldn't take that from me. But what's worse, he enjoyed putting my reputation at risk, especially with others who hold respectable positions in the industry, by releasing that private video. It definitely wasn't sexual. He's like rich guys or musicians who meet a girl, develop a crush, and fly her all over the world on tour with them, just so they can conveniently fuck them while they go from venue to venue. This guy has the money and resources to do anything he wants, and this is the path he chooses.

He wanted to feel like he'd made me so it was more satisfying when he tried to break my career—and me when he released that tape.

This is how he gets off.

It's a power fetish.

It was never Dominick I needed to blame or worry about. It was always X.

And until I know what to do, the best thing to do isn't to let him think he's won, but to let him think this doesn't bother me. That will keep me in his thoughts.

If the cat thinks the mouse is dead, it finds another mouse to play with. I need him to stay close for now.

Because I am not done with Mr. X yet. And he needs to know that he can't scare me away. Men like that feed off of fear, they crave it like a drug. If you give it to them, they want more and more and will do whatever it takes for an even bigger, better reaction the next time when the novelty's worn off. No one is feasting upon me unless I want them to.

And if there are other people watching me right now, I'm going to give them something to watch, other than my knees knocking together in fear. Whatever will be, will be, whether I'm terrified or not.

Might as well enjoy myself.

The guy whose cock I had in my hand is back at the bar, and I grab him by the hand and pull him to another room, hoping no one's already in it.

I need to use him to feel better, to feel back in control of something, even if only for a moment. And sometimes the best way to lose control is by giving yours up.

The room has a shiny black harness in it, hooked up to a few hooks in the ceiling ready to go. My partner strips my clothes from my body and puts me in the harness, strapping me in like a pony ready to pull a wagon. I'd better get plowed or I'm going to whip this motherfucker.

I spread my legs, inserting them through the loops so they land around the tops of my thighs and spread my legs wide open, baring my pussy, making me dangle in the air. He raises my hands above my head, looping more leather straps around my wrists and elbows so I'm fastened tightly to the harness, ready to be swung however he wants me to be. I see everything in the reflection in front of me—and know it's a two-way mirror.

It's not just so we can watch ourselves. It's never that prosaic, is it?

From my lower vantage point, I can see his cock straining at his pants again, and my mouth waters at the sight of it. It feels like it's been forever since I fucked.

He strips for me, taking his time, rubbing that cock up the inside of my thigh and down the other, not letting it touch my pussy lips. He slips behind me and I watch us in the mirror as he teases my nipples, jutting out from the way my arms are above my head, and I get wetter and wetter, watching the way my labia start to glisten with longing.

Watching yourself do something like fucking is always a surprise the first few times. Catching sight of your own face when you come is enough to make you want to practice in the mirror for a while before the next time. Most of us are weird-looking when we peak. Sometimes people look shocked, like the orgasm hit them by surprise even though they felt it building for however long they were fucking—and that was the goal the whole time. Others smile, looking so damned happy to be there getting their genitals wet that their faces stretch into goofy grins that seem so out of place. Mostly people seem angry. Sex isn't pretty. But it's hot.

Same with musicians. Have you ever seen a guitar player when he's really into his playing? Lip biting, face scrunched, head shaking. Singers can make the silliest faces of all, contorting their muscles like it's a contest. Double chins form when aiming for a low note, eyes widened as far as they'll go when straining for the high ones. Blues singers make faces like they smell something terrible, but we love it.

But it's art. Art isn't always pretty, but it's profound and sexy and powerful.

Then he surprises me by crouching and licking my pussy with one long stroke of his flattened tongue. I jump at the way his mouth almost burns me after the air has cooled my vulva down, even as I was wet and spread and ready for whatever he wanted to give me.

Held like this, the only part of him touching me is his mouth. His hot tongue poking around my clit like a micro phallus with good intentions but bad aim. Yet, it feels good. The straps dig into the skin where my thighs meet my ass. It's strange being suspended this way, untethered to the world, to a bed, to everything but the licking and sucking of this stranger who's trying to make me feel good.

There's a big difference between having sex with someone you're attracted to and making love to someone you love and trust. Sometimes you're more willing to take risks with someone when you don't think the sex act will have ramifications in regards to the equilibrium of the relationship going forward. Power shifts in the bedroom can have changes when outside it. They shouldn't, and probably wouldn't, but it's all about perception.

Men, if you wanted to be pegged, would you ask your girlfriend, or would you be worried she might think you wanted to bottom and have sex with a man?

Ladies, would you ask him to fuck you in his little sister's bed, or would you worry he might think you were into something a little kinkier than you were going for and would look at you differently?

Asking a stranger you're never going to see again to do those things can be much easier because you don't care. You can fuck their brains out and then happily move on without worrying about the fallout. You don't have to think, *If I tell him I want him to choke me and make me call him daddy, that it's only this one time and only in the bedroom, I don't want to submit to him any other time.*

Funny how sometimes it's easier to be real with strangers.

Then again, the depth of connection that comes only when we know and love and trust our partners is something to experience as well. Having the person who knows what you love without having to ask, you know you're totally safe letting go with. The one who you know won't ever let you get hurt, and would never do anything to put you in harm's way. That comfort that feels like coming home, that transcends the physical into something closer to spiritual and emotional when your bodies join together.

When you're not fucking, but making love.

Not much can touch the intensity of that.

But, the heightened awareness of being tied up and at a stranger's mercy while on a compound on an island in Central America comes close.

I can't even squeeze his head between my thighs as I thrash around against his mouth, desperate to come, craning my neck so I can see my wetness coating his face as he buries it between my thighs.

There's a flicker of movement behind the two-way mirror—or maybe it's a blood vessel pulsing in the corner of my vision in time with my pulse, quickening as my partner does a spiral and a thrust of his fingers. Someone could be watching. Watching this man eat me, watching the expression on my face as he does. I lick my lips as he licks mine.

I like being able to see my face. Seeing what they see as they watch, possibly getting themselves off to this.

Pressure builds inside me, and my head tips back.

But a part of me is unable to relax as Mr. X's words echo in my mind. Not quite a boast but a threat.

# SEVENTEEN

✀

I'M SITTING AT THE BAR of a club sipping a heavily limed soda water through a tiny black straw. I was walking home after a training session with Penelope when I passed this place.

The music drew me in, but when I got inside I saw it was a live orchestra, only they play electronic instruments instead of the acoustic and it's over a pulsating beat. Sort of like Dvorak Drum N Bass. Modern and classical all at once, and it's insistent and impossible to tune out once you hear it. They're interesting to see as well, dressed up like undead Victorian fops complete with wigs and buckles on their shoes.

I like it here.

It's not huge. The walls are black and the ceiling and floor are blinding white, almost glossy enough to see yourself in. It gives the impression of being a limitless space, never ending, with motion above and below from the ceiling and floor, as though there are crowds of spirits teeming beneath the surface of both, unable to break through. It brings to mind purgatory, for obvious reasons. We in the bar are waiting to see our final destination.

Above or below.

It smells like sweat and smoke and something else, as though aromatic oils have been left burning for ten minutes too long. Sweet, but scorched. A hint of spoil through the freshness only adds to the atmosphere.

There's a young woman laid out on a platform off to the side but not against the wall. She's surrounded by about ten people, the star of the semi-private show, but she seems terrified. I move closer for a better look. Her arms shake and she makes these pathetic little mewling sounds that grate up and down my spine.

I want her to get over whatever this is and relax into the experience, relax into her deepest desires. This place isn't for everyone, it's a hard won privilege to be here, and she's squandering it. It's not like anyone here is going to murder her. I've seen the darkest side of this society, and everything is consensual. The only victims in this place are willing ones, going along with the illusion, but everyone has a safeword.

This compound gives the illusion of danger, but no one here really wishes harm on anyone else...other than Mr. X. But this place is safe, though not private, and she needs to get over her fears if she's going to get anywhere in life.

Honestly, who even brought this little neophyte here? I creep closer, annoyed with her lack of gratitude which doesn't seem like part of a scene.

The murmurs of the people standing around her register. They're berating her, asking how she dares to think she deserves to be here with them, insulting her—insulting everything from her appearance to her past and obvious present inexperience. I find myself leaning over her as well, joining in. It's not to break her down, it's for her to break her own limits down. Sometimes you need someone else to throw that first punch at the wall, though.

The mood suddenly shifts at a nod from a tall man with a crimson tie who is the obvious leader of this group. He begins stroking her shoulders and she relaxes at his touch, relaxes as the rest of us begin softly stroking her naked flesh in soothing motions.

I'd thought her being dramatic, but the goosebumps prove her fear is real. My scorn softens a little, gentling my touch with real care.

"What are your deepest fears?" he asks, leaning close to her. "Other than humiliation?"

"Losing control," she replies, blinking back tears.

He motions at a woman near her feet, and she ties the girl's feet apart while he ties her wrists above her head.

Interesting.

There's a giant cylindrical funnel filled with something nearby—urine—that takes me a second to realize what it is, until the girl almost pukes at the sight of it. I wonder if everyone here took a turn pissing into the top, or if one person collected urine for a few days, saving it for just this purpose. Everyone takes a handful of urine from the spigot and pours it over the woman until she's reeking with the pungent fluid and sobbing.

A few men and women have mini vibrator eggs in various bright colors, attached to strings in a bucket, and we each take a couple and drag them across her body as she shivers.

I let one hang over her neck, the weight of the vibrating egg putting pressure on her throat, but not enough to choke her, only enough to bring the potential of that to her mind. She closes her eyes and breathes more slowly, forcing herself to remain calm. Part of me wants to press harder to increase the panic, to make her confront it on a deeper level, but I don't. She's doing enough for now.

The brightly colored eggs slide all over her body, relaxing muscles, teasing flesh before we insert them inside her. We pack the tiny eggs inside her pussy and ass, tugging on the strings to jiggle them to drive her wild.

Now that she's turned on, writhing, wet inside and out, we whisper the same insults at her, blending the humiliation with the pleasure, claiming all the things we call her with a giant smile and moans.

So many moans.

We lavish attention over her, petting, rubbing, stimulating. The man who is her Master takes the vibrators from her pussy and fists her until she's writhing and screaming...and then goes beyond it into subspace with a completely blank, happy expression on her face. I smile, proud of her, seeing she's in complete bliss and no longer the scared recruit she was.

It didn't take long, but only because she finally chose to accept the experience for what it was. A gift. If she'd resisted, who knows how long we'd have stayed there. Maybe she'd have given up completely. But she broke through the fear and indecision to the pleasure and devoured it.

Those standing begin stripping and pouring urine all over her. Placing the funnel between her lips. Then a line forms at her feet of all the people who were around her in the scene. Next, she'll fuck each person one by one, covered in fluids. By the time the last person goes, the floor will be covered with puddles of urine, tears, sweat, and come.

I decide not to partake in the fucking. Though I enjoyed her and the scene, sex isn't what I came here for tonight.

I head to the bathroom. My panties are wet. I wash my hands and head back out to the bar.

While I was gone, a few new people have shown up, but one man in particular catches my eye. He's near the bar area sitting in a plush red velvet chair, with a delicate woman perched next to him in a pristine white pantsuit.

A small feast is set up in front of them as they take in the rest of the room's activities. Are they voyeurs and this is their version of a romantic meal out?

But there's something about the way they're enjoying the food, almost making a show of it. I was wrong. I thought they are voyeurs but I think they're really waiting for their moment. When my eyes are on them, the man smiles at me like he was waiting for an audience.

He picks up an oyster and a small knife, working the blade between the halves of the shell to free the meat. Removing the top, he places the half shell with the oyster on his naked lap, wedged between his cock and balls. The woman crawls forward and slurps the meat from the shell without using her hands. She returns to her place with juices dripping down her chin. He tenderly blots them away.

He picks up another to repeat the process, but cuts himself with the shell and bleeds, but the woman is not scared by the blood. She takes his finger and presses the cut to her chest above her heart, leaving a perfect little crimson stain on her perfectly clean top, feeding him the offending oyster with her other hand while he leisurely strokes his cock beneath the table.

They are making a show of it. *This* is what gets them off. The endless varieties of fetishes that exist in the world never ceased to surprise and delight me. There truly is something for everyone.

The way they so obviously love food in an erotic way reminds me a little of the Japanese film *Tampopo* by Juzo Itami. I wonder if they've seen it.

It's not something I've ever thought about doing, or rather wanting to do—bringing food into my sex life in this way. Food to me is sustenance. It's not sexy, though it can definitely be sensual. The creamy texture of a perfectly made cheesecake. The way a ceviche can almost make your tongue hurt when it's too bright. The perfect savory crunch of crispy bacon and the smell of it wrapping you up in memories of a thousand breakfasts of your youth.

Food is sensual. It can transport you back in time to the first time you tried a particular dish—or the last time. You remember what you were eating when your partner took you out to lunch to break up with you in a public place. You can't forget the terrible blandness of the egg salad sandwiches at your grandmother's funeral, but it was fitting because you loved her and she was gone and the day was tinged with dullness anyways.

French fries shared with best friends in high school. Mom's famous pot roast every Sunday. Fresh baked bread's unforgettable aroma from the bakery you pass every morning on the way to work. It's sensate and permeates literally every day of our lives. Some people overindulge, others obsess over having too much, and restrict themselves out of fixation or necessity. But we can't live without it.

And yet, it can be sexy as well. Who hasn't had a chocolate-covered strawberry hand fed to them by a lover eager for them to swallow it and kiss the juice from their lips? How many of us have had warm chocolate sauce poured over our bodies and licked off? Maybe a cool shot of whipped cream from a can because that's much easier to get out of the sheets in the laundry the next day. Hell, there's even edible panties. We're voracious, insatiable, starving for nourishment, for experience.

But it's not just about what we want in the bedroom, it's also about what our partners want. Sometimes, things we'd never dreamed of trying, or wanting to try, become…titillating, when we think of doing them with someone who is extremely receptive or turned on by that very thing. If they're that excited about it, that emotion can transfer to us. Have you ever been shy about being naked in front of a partner when the lights are on? And their attraction for you turned you on and made you forget all about your self-consciousness, didn't it? It's the same thing, though perhaps a little more extreme in this case.

I head to the bar and ask the bartender if he has any eggs. Obviously used to requests like these, he hands one over without even raising an eyebrow.

I lean in and whisper to his date and I can tell he's indulgent but wary, and fair enough. He doesn't know if I'm coming in here starting shit or going to attempt to overstep my bounds and take his date from him. Instead, the opposite is true. I want to give them an experience—mostly him, as it seems like he's the true food fetishist at this table. He won't enjoy it if his date doesn't know what I'm going for, so I tell her what's going to happen.

Her eyes widen with delight, and she nods, indicating for me to continue.

I crack the egg sharply against the tabletop and stick my thumb-nails inside the fractured shell, carefully pulling it in halves before letting the white drip down to the shiny black tabletop, knowing it will make a mess for them to play with later, looking like semen for them to leave or flake off the table as may be their wont to do.

With my fingers, I finish separating the yolk from the white, careful to keep the membrane intact. I make eye contact with the man before repositioning the slippery ball farther down on my fingertips and then tipping my head back and slipping it into my mouth.

It's cool with surprisingly little flavor, and gives on my tongue, flattening a little. I lean close to the man's date, and slowly let the yolk slide from my mouth into hers, making sure to keep my lips soft and my teeth out of the way so as not to break it.

She accepts it into her mouth with a sigh, putting on a bit of a show for her date, but nothing overboard. Maybe she really is into this as much as he is, I don't know. I kiss her neck, leaving a wet trail with the raw egg on my lips.

The man strokes himself faster and moans. My shoes make me a few inches taller than her, so I bend a little and caress her jaw, opening my mouth so she can deposit the yolk back inside. She moves slowly, letting the yellow ball peek through her lips for a moment before widening her mouth to let it slide inside mine again.

It's warm from her mouth or maybe mine, and now has the slight tinge of oyster from her meal I interrupted. She presses against me, rubbing her peaked little nipples against my chest, her exhalations increasing as though she can't wait for me to give the yolk back.

We do this a couple more times before I kiss her while the egg's in her mouth again. I invade her mouth with my tongue as well, and

I plunge it hard, capturing the yolk between my tongue and the roof of her mouth, tearing into the fragile membrane, pulling back before it can coat my tongue because this next part is just for them.

I lead her around the table to kneel at his feet. He inserts an index finger inside her mouth and coats her lips with the yellow silkiness before kissing her, hard, thoroughly. Yolk drips down both of their chins, coating their kiss in the silkiness of it. She kisses a yellow trail down his body to his cock.

I walk away from their table with a smile.

# EIGHTEEN

∽∾∿ᴑᴑᴑ∾∽

I WAKE UP LISTLESS, unable to go back to sleep although I'm still tired. The sun has already risen, sending ribbons of light through the holes in my blinds, cascading onto the wall beside me.

Thoughts of the conference have been preying on me, and all I can think is that whatever Mr. X is hiding has got to be huge. He's threatening me because, on some level, he's scared. But it makes me think about the things we choose to hide, the things we need to protect at any and all cost.

What secrets would you be willing to die for, to kill for?

I can't really relate to this on a fundamental level. But if it wasn't for me... If my sister or brother or best friend had seen or done something and needed my help...I mean, you hear them say that a friend will help you move, but a best friend will help you move a body. It's a cute saying, but would you really commit to doing something so dark if a loved one called you in a panic in the middle of the night?

So, maybe it's not his secret at all, but one he's keeping for someone else. I know things about people, co-workers, sources, bosses, friends, lovers, that could take them down in a well-placed article. But where's the fun in toppling someone else's house of cards when you can spend that time and energy building your own up instead?

Somehow, I can't see Mr. X as someone willing to put himself on the line in any way for someone else. Unless there was something in it for him. If it was a shared secret, maybe? Business partners, an investor. Men like him care about power. Men like him derive power from money. Hitting him in the bank account would hurt. I wonder if that's it.

Maybe it's time to explore a little more of this place. Find out from someone other than a member what the lowdown is.

I get dressed and head out. While refrigerators are stocked and needs are met, I've still seen few markets around the place. Maybe they're fronts whose sole purpose is to lend an air of authenticity. I'm not sure. But this island isn't the typical time-share. Someone's got to know something, and the powerful people who play here aren't going to be the ones to ask.

I need to make sense of everything. People stay here, wallow in the decadence, but do they live here year round? How are their businesses maintained? In today's era, where most of what we do is communicated in binary, I suppose one would be able to exist entirely online and be able to run a corporation.

I walk down the street, looking at each villa as I walk past, but not making it obvious that I'm assessing them. Nothing here could possibly cost less than eight figures, maybe more, but down here I imagine building places like this would cost less with the exchange rate on the local currency.

I'm thinking of what I saw when I landed in Honduras, the sheer poverty that was around. Countries devastatingly poor like this aren't the exception, and it's hard to say which is worse than another when you factor in the variables like GDP, women's rights, human corruption, natural disasters, diseases. People die in so many ways in places like this, and the world keeps on turning as though it's not happening.

It's difficult to focus on making the world around you a better place when you're barely surviving in it.

But look around the globe. America's part of the problem simply because of tourism.

We're bargain hunters, always hungry for that deal, searching for the place where we can feel like we're rock stars when we go to spend our hard-earned cash. And, we like to go to exotic places. So these countries oblige our greed. They create resorts in slums, luxury right next to poverty and no one caring. People brag about going to see slums of other countries so that they can go home feeling better about their lot in life, as though savoring their privilege. As though the grief and difficulties of the natives of those places provides them with some sort of sick, twisted inspiration to keep on trucking in their nine to five.

It's sick and rampant and we've all done it. Even here in this private place, set up to be the ultimate fantasy, you can't even see outside the high walls. I guess seeing the regular people struggling along in their daily lives down here is a real mood killer.

I head inside the little market on the corner I find, grabbing a fresh mango on the way inside as an excuse. A beautiful local boy, maybe seventeen, smiles at me and greets me with a shy but wide grin. I wonder if he's a paid actor, hired to maintain the illusion that this is truly a world unto itself, or if he belongs to someone. Does he get abused here? Used here? Is he happy? What does he want from his life, for his life? Does he have the freedom to go after his dreams, if he has any, or is he trapped by a world not his making?

"Miss?" His smile falters. "Are you all right?"

I realize I've been staring. But it makes me think what it would be like to have a city that was run like a private fiefdom, operating beyond the law, outside of the codes that govern social, moral, and even sexual behavior. Or even somewhere like the Vatican, where all kinds of crimes and intrigues have gone on behind closed doors for centuries, and nobody is any the wiser or able to offer up any proof that they even occurred because the cover-ups are so damn airtight. Part of me panics for this boy, desperately worried about his future.

"Are you happy?"

He frowns as though puzzled by the context of my question, or at the words themselves. Has anyone ever asked him before? He looks around and I notice how clean the store is, as though it is a movie set, or like someone has too many hours on their hands and spends time polishing endlessly because that is their life.

His lips part.

"Catherine. Good morning." The familiar voice comes from behind me just before I feel a hand rest on my shoulder.

"Good morning, Mr. X. How are you today?" the boy asks, snapping to an alert interest, bordering obsequiousness.

The slightest hint of annoyance crosses Mr. X's features, but he ignores the boy and stares down at me.

I'm confused for a moment that he's taller today before realizing I was wearing heels during our last encounter and sandals today. "Morning," I return, for it is morning. I'll reserve the qualifier for later.

"Have you thought any more about what I said?"

"About writing a slanted article?"

He presses his lips into a thin smile. "I do so like your directness. Yes, about writing the article that's in both of our best interests."

"I've been thinking about it, yes. It's been difficult to focus on much else with the way you delivered your threat."

"That wasn't a threat." He tilts his head and it amazes me how he can turn on the boyish charm when it suits him. "And I know it affected your focus. I saw you the other night."

So I'd been right to continue on as though I was unbothered by his confessions.

I shrug.

"And what conclusions have you come up with, Catherine?"

"I'm wildly curious about what it is, exactly, that I'll be writing about in regards to this conference. I looked online and information wasn't easily procured. I'm not going to lie, it bothers me. But," I hedge, "I also know that going up against a man such as yourself isn't something many people do. I get the sense it isn't smart."

"Indeed."

"And since I already know of two women, Inana and Anna, who you've...gotten rid of? I'll be watching my step very carefully."

"Yes. And good. Keep those pretty little toes inside the lines I've drawn for you and everything will be fine. You could be the next Gina Lollobrigida." He gives me a radiant grin and leaves.

Gina Lollobrigida was the actress turned photojournalist who scored the interview with Fidel Castro in the seventies. She's lived a long and happy life, even dated Sinatra for a while, instead of turning into a tragic cautionary tale like some of her contemporaries. I'm sure Mr. X doesn't care about her charitable work, donating millions to stem cell research and Italian American causes.

He's not saying I could be successful in transitioning to another career the way I would like.

His point is that she's still alive.

Not wanting to be anywhere near him, but needing to get the hell away, I head outside and turn the opposite direction, walking as fast as I'm able while still appearing casual.

It's the perfect day in paradise. Birds are singing, the sky is a blue so pure it looks fake. The gardens are perfectly maintained, not even a twig out of place. The temperature is in the eighties and bearable. If this was a vacation I'd paid for, I'd be singing the resort's praises on a review online somewhere.

I stroll along, gently swinging my arms and keeping a pleasant smile on my face.

Underneath it all, I'm wondering how I can get information from him about the truth—and write what I need to write.

But I don't even know what that is yet. How can I fight him when I don't know what his strengths are, or what I can use to sink him with it? Because there's no way in hell I'm writing his little one-sided ego-stroke, or alibi, or whatever it is he wants me to fabricate.

I start to feel hot, so I veer off the path into a perfect little green space and rest on a bench, looking up at the sky as though I'll find some answers there. It's like I'm sinking through the ground with the water coming through the sprinklers in a fine mist.

I never really wanted to be a reporter. I feel the weight of burden swoop in my stomach. It's heavy and I need to purge it, give whatever it is to the world and let them be the ones to bring him to justice. I can't, and that knowledge is starting to make me panic. I want to scream and get it out, make him suffer for ruining my escape from my past.

My past. Of course it had to have been Mr. X who leaked the tape, but that means we're more connected than I thought, share more history and mutual friends—if a man like him is capable of having friends. As a member, he could easily have been at the party in the mansion that night and filmed me having sex with DeVille. He's sick enough to have released it to get me to agree to doing his article.

But why me? What is it about me that he's seen and fixated on?

I don't want this. I want to explore this life, but one where he's not here orchestrating chess moves when I didn't notice I'd wandered onto the board.

I'm tired of the game.

# NINETEEN

PAIN IN MY WRISTS SNAPS me from sleep with a jolt. Not pain. Pressure.

Hands.

Strange hands on my wrists, pinning them to the mattress.

Two male silhouettes in the dark and the masculine scent of them both, musky and woodsy. Two men in my bedroom.

Mr. X.

I suck in a deep breath, but before I can scream out at the man holding my hands down, another presses his hand over my mouth. His fingers don't cover my nostrils but they smell of lime like he just squeezed a wedge of it into a drink. Maybe he did; his breath is sweet like cola.

I struggle. It's futile. Adrenaline courses through my body, more effective than any drug I could have taken to bring clarity and awareness and fear, heightening my senses.

On a normal day it would take a good hour and three cups of coffee to bring me to this level of alertness. Fear is the great equalizer: I'm as awake as my assailants who tug me from the bed and onto my feet. I stumble, but they hold me tightly.

I shouldn't have underestimated Mr. X. But I never thought he'd try to hit me on the island where I have friends. In my own home. So soon, before I had the chance to betray him, disobey his bullshit orders, but then again that's the definition of the best time to strike—before your opponent has the chance to sink your ship.

I pull hard, using my bodyweight to try and fall and catch them off guard, frantic to escape the men's grasp, and the one covering my mouth moves to take my other arm, sandwiching me at their sides as they manhandle me down the hallway.

It takes me a moment to process that my mouth is now uncovered. "Who the hell are you?" I demand.

"Javier."

"Paul."

Their direct answers surprise me, and I stop struggling for a moment and let them march me down the hallway. "Why are you here?"

"We cannot say," they reply in unison.

But why are they answering me at all? "Let me go," I try.

They comply, releasing my arms but staying close, not moving from my side. I scramble away a few steps, trying to integrate this.

How very fucking strange. It's as though they're obeying me.

I cross my arms, still unsure and vulnerable and not enjoying the feeling in the slightest. I point at the one who called himself Paul. "Stand over there." I gesture down the hallway.

He strides to the place I indicated without asking why.

"You too," I tell Javier.

And he does.

I quickly rub the sleep from my eyes, wondering if this is a bizarre dream, but I know it isn't.

They stand there, fifteen feet from me, and my heart finally slows down so it no longer throbs in my ears. I flip on the light to get a better look at their faces.

It's then I notice how young—and attractive—they are, and also the fact that they're wearing nothing but little black shorts. Not quite boxer briefs. Bare feet.

What kind of kidnappers don't wear shoes?

Paul bites his lip and Javier appears to be suppressing a smile. These guys are either the weirdest fucking rapists or murderers ever…or that's not why they're here at all. They're here for a reason, though.

I stand taller, growing more certain who actually sent these boys my way. They're no older than twenty-five, but I'd say they're twenty-one or twenty-two. They seem like they're waiting…for me. Penelope had to have sent them, but for what purpose? Why would they wake me up that way? "Are you here to fuck me?"

They shrug.

Interesting.

"What is it that you're here to do?" I ask. They look at each other then back at me and shrug again.

This reeks of a test. They're here for something and answer direct questions…for the most part. They obeyed when I told them to…is that it?

They're here to do whatever I say, like, what, personal sex slaves? I must admit, I find the idea sexy. That must be it. They've done everything I've told them to do. Nothing more and nothing less.

And instead of submitting, I realize I am meant to take the power back and dominate the hell out of these two men.

I thought Penny was teaching me to sub and what to expect from each toy when really it was about learning to dominate. But she had to frame it like that because you can't order someone to be a Dominant—they have to know that's what they are, what they want, and want it badly enough to latch onto it from within before they can take the crop in hand. I looked at it as something I'd done a few times and thoroughly enjoyed, but never really internalized it as part of my identity. Is it what I want?

I think back, remembering. I remember a room in Max's hotel, with a young man whose lips were a little too red. I remember his beautiful vulnerability when he let me tie him to the bedposts and mark him with a rod—arms, thighs, belly. He'd wanted me to hurt him, and so I had.

My nipples tighten and I close my eyes. Line after line, I enjoyed the redness that sprang up until he was like a tiger or a zebra I'd created, one slap of the rod at a time, as he'd cried tears of joy and relief.

I open my eyes now and look at my boys who want the same thing. It felt strange to be the one giving orders and yet I'd taken to it, because something about it was strangely comforting. Yet I abandoned it so quickly afterwards. Why?

I'd want to discover what his limits are.

The lines I made on his skin were warm on my tongue.

I lost myself in the surrealism of the scene, in the sadistic person that man wanted me to be, taking joy in causing him pain. I turned into claws and hurt and teeth and sharpness, and I was a razor's edge away from flaying the meat of us both from our bones just to see if we were the same inside when Max stepped into the room and pulled me off the man.

I impressed the shit out of him that night by losing myself.

Is that it? If I gave in fully to the Catherine that came out to play that night, does that mean I'd forever be altered? Could it be that I wasn't ready at the time?

Am I ready now?

Is it that I've been shrinking away from this side of myself because I'm scared of what I'll become? Scared of being selfish and doing exactly what I want to do without waiting for someone to do it first? Being the action instead of the reaction?

I'm understanding now that this is basically Penny's way of provoking me into realizing that. But now, it's deeper. Now it's not just sex, it's about controlling a room with nothing more than my will and imagination.

"Follow me," I direct them, heading to my playroom where all the toys I could dream up are at my disposal. Their feet make eager little slaps on the tile floors as they hurry to do what they're told.

I flip on the light and survey the room. So many toys and so little time.

But what should I have these two men do to me?

Maybe the best thing isn't what they can do to me.

"Paul, give me the purple vibrator from that cupboard." I point to it. He grabs it and gives it to me, his eyes lighting up as I strip my panties off and take a seat on a bench a few feet away where I can better enjoy the show they're going to give me.

"Take your shorts off, boys."

They do. I rev up the vibrator, touching my nipples with it before bringing it to my clit, rubbing it between my legs for a moment while watching their eyes grow hungry and their cocks swell with interest.

"I know you're here for my enjoyment. For my pleasure. And I want you two to have a great time too." I work the tip against my clit. "But I think I've got something a little different in mind than whoever sent you. See, I don't want you to fuck me. I want you to fuck each other," I say, enjoying the matching looks of realization that hit their faces.

Something profound sings inside my blood, making my veins hum with an energy I can barely contain. *This* is what I've been missing out on the past few years and not just the bedroom. I've been waiting for external things to shape my life when all along I should have molded it more into what I wanted. In business and in pleasure.

I could make these men do anything to each other, I bet. Maybe not maim or kill, but things could get delightfully indecent if I choose.

I practically purr at the thought—or rather, the vibrator does my purring for me.

I arch my brows at them both. "Kiss."

The single syllable reverberates through my playroom like thunder, and they obey, lips meeting with such force I know it's got to hurt, but they bury their hands in the other's hair and keep going. Men kiss each other differently than women do. It's never as soft, never as self-conscious.

I smile, an idea skipping around my head. "I want you two to fuck like you hate each other."

The energy in the room shifts as their hands find places to grab and hold, roughly, contemptuously claiming each other. They glare into each other's eyes as they furiously stroke their cocks, close enough that their balls rub together. It's heady and hot, making them do whatever I want.

I plunge the vibrator deep inside my soaking pussy and hold it there. "Paul, eat Javier's asshole. Javier, let me hear how good it feels."

They drop to their knees on the floor and Javier spreads, letting out a string of curses and sighs when Paul's tongue finds his puckered hole.

"Javier, suck Paul's cock. And drag your teeth just a little."

Javier grins and complies, and soon Paul is gasping and his hips are bucking.

I fuck myself hard with the vibrator. "I want to see my favorite number. Sixty-nine!"

They scramble into position, heads bobbing up and down, tongues dancing over heads, and it's fucking gorgeous. I pull the vibrator out just before I come.

"Paul, come fuck my pussy." I know I said they were going to fuck each other—and they are. But I want in on this action too.

Paul strides over and slams his cock home inside my wet hole, primed from the vibrator. Javier watches and I smile at him. "What are you waiting for? Paul's ass isn't going to fuck itself, darling." I reach between Paul and me, wetting my hand with my come, and turning him around to slather my arousal between his cheeks.

Javier uses it for lube, pushing into Paul as Paul pushes back inside of me. Javier sets a punishing pace that sets the tone for Paul's thrusts and soon I'm coming with a scream, pussy rippling around his cock like a jazz pianist's fingers dancing up and down the keys.

I push Paul's chest. "Off."

He pulls out of me with a wet slap. "Javier, come."

He grips Paul's hips hard and pulls him back, sheathing himself completely and coming in about four deep thrusts as Paul's cock gets harder, his prostate being pummeled.

I give him a second before ordering Paul to fuck Javier as hard as he can.

Paul smiles and does, semen dripping from his ass as he fills Javier with hot spurts of cream. Now they both have slippery cheeks.

"Lick each other clean," I order, wanting to see them eat their own come, getting even wetter when they actually do it.

Fuck me, that's sexy. I don't know why straight guys are so dainty about it. "Now kiss."

They do, and this time it's with more passion, more tenderness.

I'm filled with power, but exhaustion has started to creep into the afterglow. Besides, they did so well. "Carry me to the bathroom." They make a cradle from their arms, and carry me upstairs to the master bath. I look at the tub. "Well?"

Paul runs the water while Javier pours in some rosewater he finds in the cupboard. When it's prepared, they help me into it.

I wave a hand at them. "Off you go. You're dismissed. Lock the door on the way out, boys. And tell whoever it was that sent you that I am very pleased."

They kiss my hands and smile softly at me before obeying.

Spent, I lie back in the tub, wet and satisfied and feeling more powerful than I have in a long time.

I feel ready for anything.

# TWENTY

REPORTERS GET INVITED ALONG TO conferences so they can see firsthand what's happening to the indigenous people in the area. Honduras isn't without its share of issues. I'm aware there are political issues surrounding environmental and humanitarian issues with the new development I'm here to investigate....but with the way Mr. X has been threatening me, it's got to be something bigger and darker than this.

The hotel has done the best it could with what it had, but you can tell the grand ballroom here gets used next to never by the way the staff have matching expressions that are slightly pinched with exhaustion. Also, sometimes they have to look around for a minute before directing you to A or B, as though they only learned the layout of the rooms ten minutes ago themselves. As "barely suitable" as this place is for men like these, it's good enough, and the way they swell with self-import bothers me. I swear, if I hear the words "tacky" or "backwater" one more time… If they hate this place so much, they should have chosen somewhere else.

Still, it's not like the attendees could build their own venue just for a place they're meeting at one time.

They could, but they won't. That would leave something behind for the people of the region, and the only time people like this give anything to others is when there's a photo op involved to make them look good. Besides, their wives are usually the ones in charge of the charitable donations. It gives them something to do, other than cultivating their pill-popping and shoe collections.

The rooms are slightly too cold to allow for the expensive suits because God forbid one of these powerful men be seen in even slightly casual clothing—or seen breaking a sweat. They're worse than women wearing a full face of waterproof makeup to the pools, scared of sweating or washing it off, so they keep their faces above the water while having "fun" with the kids in the terrified off-chance that someone snaps a casual photo of the family.

It's probably also a sign of wealth or prestige that they can keep the air conditioning going at full clip when in a country as sweltering with poverty as with the heat and humidity. Hopefully the hotel is getting paid a little extra for this luxury. I should look into that.

I don't know every person in attendance, although there are quite a few I'm familiar with. Then again, businessmen tend to blend together with their similarly expensive suits, haircuts, and accessories. Even their behaviors and mannerisms paint them with a similar brush and blur the lines of individuality.

I'm hoping that the whiskey in their glasses will encourage loose lips a little later on—not that any of these men are lightweights when it comes to liquor. Building up tolerances is what politicians and businessmen do best. Tolerance to the suffering of others, to the needs of others as well as to alcohol.

They speak in hushed voices, controlled so passersby can't hear conversations—though undoubtedly want to—except for when they're laughing too loud. You only hear what they want you to hear. It's so annoyingly political and utterly bland, but innately sinister, gatherings like this one. It's the kind of event where you'd inevitably come across a rock star fist-bumping the world's power elite as they plan new wars and solidify strategies to rape the world of its riches and natural resources.

Of course, nothing that interesting actually happens at conferences. Not that I've seen, anyways.

I see a representative, one of the partners at that corporation—you know, the big one everyone freaks out about when it comes to genetically modified foods. I was in an elevator with him once, and he was actually one of the nicest men I've encountered at a conference. Polite, well-mannered, didn't hit on me or try to intimidate me. There's a lot of fear mongering when it comes to what we put into our bodies.

I think it's a distraction and that company is a scapegoat to misdirect us from what's really happening. There's always a darker picture if you flip the painting around.

About ten companies own nearly one hundred percent of the world's food brands. Everything from the generic store brands to the luxury items you find in your grocery store. It's insane. Go look in your cupboard right now and look at all the "different" brands you buy on a regular basis, showing support with your hard-earned cash.

X brand is cheaper, but Y doesn't use hormones. Brand X is more expensive, but brand Y isn't made from concentrate—and that's better, right?

You think you're buying from a smaller company with higher standards for the products and more ethical beliefs and practices when really they've been swallowed up by one of the bigger brands years ago and you're still ultimately supporting one of the bad guys with your wallet regardless of your choice. More like the illusion of choice because sometimes they'll even pit their own brands against each other to see which the consumers choose regionally.

But the same water that makes a Coke or a Pepsi also makes the juice you drink in the morning—unless you're freshly squeezing the fruit from your own back yard. Your healthy choices may not be as healthy as you think, or as "natural." Big companies aren't innately evil, though there's more opportunity for corruption on a large scale. At the top of those ten companies are boards or committees. And at the head of that board or committee is one person. You go high up enough and there's always one person calling the shots. Everyone knows that.

So, basically, ten people control what we're all consuming. I think that's too much power for someone to have. But you rarely hear about this. All we're, pardon the pun, fed are the buzzwords we've been taught. Avoid Genetically Modified. Gravitate to organic, or grain fed. Free-range. Gluten-free. All natural! But some of the worst substances are organic and all natural. Buzzwords don't make things less dangerous to put inside our bodies.

I'm not saying organic is bad. It's a business, like any other. I'm just saying to educate yourself about where things come from. "Organic" doesn't mean "pesticide-free," but that's one of those truths that we've all come to believe as fact even though it's misinformation. Those ten companies are banking on our ignorance, but it's not malevolent. It's business.

And, sadly, business is the most impersonal thing of all. We're taught to grant latitude to those who stab us in the backs in the name of business deals. It's only business. It's competition. You'd have done the same thing if the tables were turned.

But would you?

I wander around, invisible to the men here except for my legs and breasts which they stare at. No one makes eye contact, which is sort of hilarious to me while being offensive as well. Clearly, I am not even the sum of my parts to these guys—I'm just…my parts.

Bits of conversations filter through the din of the meeting, but nothing that makes me sit up and take notice. It's mostly bullshitting and schmoozing at this stage. There will be a few presentations later—maybe that's when I'll learn something new.

I've often wondered how differently events like these would be if I came in flawless drag, dressed as a man. Would conversations halt when I approached a circle then as they do now? Would I be able to engage and be taken seriously instead of patronized and spoken over? Maybe that could be a good social commentary piece. Then again, it's not like it's anything new. Women already know all about this and men would continue to reject the premise that in certain circles we get treated way differently simply for our gender.

I circulate, trying to keep moving, but not so I seem to be zinging around the place or have an agenda, when I stop in my tracks.

Mr. X.

I recognize the half-profile I see of him and part of me wants to turn him by the shoulders so I can check out his nametag and see what it says instead of the mysterious initial he's shared with me. More likely, he's not even wearing a nametag. The egos of pompous, self-important men like him couldn't bear to dream that someone may not know exactly who they are. It's unlikely he'd cause a scene, but he'd want to talk to me, to press the issue for sure. And if people see me with him, that will naturally taint the way they see me—and then I'll be unable to go unnoticed.

Think about it: if you see a stranger smiling and chatting with someone you don't get along with, you automatically treat them a little more warily than you would have if you'd first met them in the same situation but with a group of your friends. Birds of a feather, and all that. It's not fair, but it is what it is, as they say. Besides, people may recognize me as a reporter and be wary of speaking to him as freely, choosing to relegate their communications with him to emails and phone calls to avoid me seeing their connections.

I'm invisible now, able to get close enough to overhear conversations because I'm just an unassuming, sweet little thing. All that will change if one of the men condescends to speak to me. Because then the rest of them might think I'm somebody too and realize that I am. *You're damn right I am.*

Every question I ask from that point on might as well be coming from Mr. X's mouth. I can't let that happen. I need unbiased information, but my face is flushed and I can't seem to focus. I walk on the balls of my feet to keep my heels from clacking on the floor as I head down a hallway around the corner. There were smaller offices over here—perfect for incognito deals and private handshakes.

Mr. X seems to be upping his intimidation factor, maybe thinking that because I'm in a foreign place I will be helpless. Or, maybe he's just getting more desperate since I haven't been playing the part of intimidated girl, ready to write everything he says the way he wants it to be read.

It only proves he's got a scandalous skeleton deep inside his closet that he wants to keep there. I need to find out what he's hiding. Maybe there's sealed documents I'll get access to that show people have already been murdered for speaking out about new developments in the country. Maybe Penny knows something specific, or could at least point me in the direction of another businessman here who would talk to me, someone with a grudge of their own against Mr. X. Why didn't I think of this before? I need to call her.

The first door in the hall I try is unlocked, and I push inside, ducking through to formulate my next move when a man rushes in with me, firmly closing the door behind us, leaving us in the dark. Alone. My pulse kicks up.

I needed to get away to think, to call Penelope to see if she knows anything specific, and here he is inside the room with me. Mr. X saw me and is here. Now what?

I flick on the light, wanting to not feel so vulnerable in the dark, wanting to let him see the determination on my face when I confront him…only it's not Mr. X.

"What are you doing here?" I ask in surprise.

Deville smiles.

# TWENTY-ONE

"I'M HERE TO GET SOME real work done while my double is on vacation with Geena in the states."

At least he's honest. Strange to think he's got a double out there, taking boring holiday snaps with the wife while he's really out here. And somehow no one notices. Was he on the compound too with the rest of The Juliette Society members? Is this what happens? Does he get away from it all to refill on debauchery to spare his precious, fragile, suitable-as-First-Lady wife the attention she'd never know what to do with?

I really don't want to know the finer details of their sex life.

I am curious, though, as to how often people like DeVille make use of the private community. Is it a once a year thing, or do some permanently live there? Do they stop by whenever they're in the area? I was going to ask Penelope but it slipped my mind.

Instead, I ask him how often he comes down here and he smirks. "Is that a pickup line?"

The energy between us shifts, suddenly, like the charge that fills the air before a thunderstorm. It's electric and intense.

Remembering how it was the last time I saw him with the double—and fueled by the fear and tension now, I find myself moving forward into his space. When we were fucking, I still don't know which Bob was actually him. I don't know who I kissed, who fucked my pussy, who fucked my ass. They touched me the same way, looked at me the same way.

The same way he's looking at me now.

He's always had this charisma that politicians and movie stars have. The kind that makes you focus on their best features and forget about their less than perfect ones. It helps them charm their way into pants and out of trouble.

Our mouths meet, all rough tongue and sharp teeth and pent-up aggression. I kiss him, turned on at us getting hot and heavy in someone's office while some of the most influential men in the world are outside this door. While Mr. X is outside this door.

I sink into the comfort of having this powerful man putting his hands on me out of desire, knowing his weaknesses, his strengths. Knowing that right now, I'm the one in the position of power because I know his secrets.

And never told them.

He trusts me.

He shouldn't.

He's literally fucked me and fucked me over, and yet here we are, pressed up against each other, hands roving over clothes and curves and edges like young lovers five minutes until curfew.

Strangely, the first thing that floods my mind isn't how he felt inside me the last time I saw him. "I used to have a fantasy about Jack and me in your office."

Bob's teeth lightly abrade my neck. "Oh? What was it?"

I tip my head back, grinning at what I thought was a real fantasy—but that was before I'd kicked my imagination's limits in the ass. "I'd have worn something under a trench coat. Heels. Stockings and garters. Sometimes I was naked beneath it, wearing nothing but red lipstick."

"A lot of windows in that office."

"I know."

Deville grinds his hard cock against me. "Then what?"

"I'd push him backwards into your leather swivel chair, and we'd fuck right there."

"That's the fantasy? I have to say, Catherine, that's a little disappointing." He bites my shoulder and I press harder against his mouth, liking the way it feels. "I thought you had a better imagination than that."

I smile. "I was going to boss him around a little first. To be a good boy and watch as I stripped."

His cock is bulging, tenting out the fabric of his boxer briefs when he unbuttons his pants and pushes them slightly down. He turns me around so my breasts press against the mahogany paneled wall and the scent of orange oil fills my nostrils. I spread my legs as far as my skirt will allow. It's not far enough.

Stiff fabric is a real mood killer.

He slides it up to my waist and runs his fingers over the pantyhose, up and down my seam where my thong dips between my ass cheeks before reaching inside the tights and tugging my thong to the side.

I expect his cock to spear my soaking little hole, but instead, I feel his warm breath on my inner thigh, then his tongue lapping at my cunt from behind.

The movements of his tongue are slightly abrasive through the fabric of the hosiery, but in a good way, dulling the direct contact but also turning the experience into something slightly unfamiliar and rough, making my nerve endings snap into awareness. I spread my legs, greedy for more.

His neck must be craned at a frightening angle to cup my clit with the tip of his tongue the way it is. I turn to see, but his face is buried in my crack, so I grab a handful of his hair and grind my hips to let him know I like what he's doing.

He works the seam of the crotch against me like a pleasant little speedbump, back and forth, before jamming his fingers up inside me, the fabric scratching at the inside of my pussy for a few thrusts before his fingers tear through. Suddenly freed, they pop up and his fingertips hit the mouth of my cervix and make me jump with their unexpected depth.

I hate that I can't finger fuck myself this deeply. Women don't have the leverage to do this to ourselves the way others can do it to us. Maybe circus contortionists or gymnasts can do it, but the average woman is at a distinct disadvantage when it comes to this aspect of masturbation.

I wonder if anyone will notice the scent of orange oil and come on me when I go back outside.

If anyone walked in right now would they recognize Bob, recognize me? Or would they assume I was another brainless little intern trying to screw her way to the top, not realizing that it would never work because I'm not ruthless enough to stay up there even if I managed to stick around for ten minutes? No, whoever opened the door would close it, not surprised this was happening, except for one key difference: I'm the one on top getting head and he's the one on his knees getting me off like it's his *joie de vivre*.

There's something to be said for standing and receiving oral. It sends the blood pumping in new and interesting ways than when you're on your back in a bed.

I lock my knees against his motions.

His fingers move faster, stroke that perfect place inside that makes me throw my head back and gasp. He spins somehow, because now his teeth press above and below my clit as he sucks it and licks and I press harder against him, wanting his neck to hurt for days after this so he remembers who it was that made it hurt while she was fucking his face like he was nothing but a toy I used and discarded.

I come hard, selfishly, not caring if he got off or gets off, only thrashing my hips harder against his face to prolong my own orgasm.

He mumbles something, or maybe he can't breathe and is trying to tell me. I don't really know or care. I lean against the wall shuddering and finally release his hair.

It's glorious.

I come back to myself a moment later, blotting my lip to take care of the sweat. I take a few steps away from him. He's cleaning himself up with a handkerchief, so he must have been jerking himself off while eating me out.

Good. I don't particularly feel like getting him, or anyone, off right now. I run my fingers through my hair and rub beneath my eyes to get rid of any smudges.

Bob stands and tucks himself back into his pants. "What is it you're doing here at the conference? Were you following me? Keeping tabs?"

I snort and strip out of my panties and hose, discarding them in a wastepaper basket nearby. The cold wetness is off-putting now that I've come and come back to reality. Besides, the men here wouldn't notice them missing anyways. If they do, that could work in my favor. "Be still, your ego."

He raises his eyebrows and I relent. "Mr. X wanted me here, told me about the conference. He's actually demanding that I write an article about it. One very biased one in his favor, of course."

He sighs. "I thought as much. Don't underestimate him."

I shrug. "I have powerful allies of my own." *And I'm not an idiot.*

He picks up on it anyways. "Catherine, you've always been a smart woman. It's one of the things I'm come to admire most about you. Don't think I'm trying to insult your intelligence by telling you to stay away from Mr. X. Trust me when I say it's not in your best interest to go against him."

That stops me in my tracks. DeVille is hesitant when it comes to this man as well? DeVille, who's in the running to be the next President of the United States, the most powerful position in our country, is wary of Mr. X? "What is it about him that has everyone so worried? No one's telling me anything." Maybe it's not something about him so much as what he's got. "What's he got on you, Bob?" I ask softly.

Bob bites the inside of his cheek and hands me a business card. "Here's my personal number in case you get into trouble."

"You're not going to the compound?" I ask, surprisingly let down at the thought of him leaving.

He smiles. "I've some other things to attend to, but shall be there in a few days."

I take the card, hoping I'll never need to use it.

# TWENTY-TWO

⌒⟋⟍⟋⟍⌒

THE CANDLES ALL BURN WITH EERIE, almost artificially red flames, no doubt achieved from placing certain chemicals in the wax that make them flicker with the unnatural hue. Fireworks are made the same way; different chemicals glow a certain shade when burned. Manganese, sulfur, barium. Beautiful, controlled explosions. Now, the monochromatic aspect gives a surreal quality to the night, painting the familiar in a strange, bloody light.

It's not dark, and yet the crimson glow makes things slightly harder to see, making the shadows deeper, more plentiful. With the masks and partygoers in such strange costumes tucked into the nooks and crevices of the mansion, it's like being in another world. I love it.

I adjust my mask—an ornate lace affair that's as light as air— careful not to touch the makeup on the lower left side of my face that makes my skin look like it's been peeled back to reveal a bright blue sky with fluffy white clouds inside, as though I'm made of sunny skies...the opposite of how I feel. My torso is also bare except for the makeup, giving the same illusion in strategic places.

I'm only a woman on the outside tonight.

An ornate handwritten invitation was fixed to my door when I got back from the conference—a surrealist ball. The perfect distraction for me after the letdown the conference turned out to be. Other than from DeVille, I got no substantial information out of anyone. Anything I did manage to glean from overheard snatches of conversation was insubstantial or irrelevant, or boring. Perhaps they were speaking in some dull code I wasn't able to decipher. Penelope didn't answer her phone, and part of me is hoping to find her here tonight as much as I'm looking forward to the diversion from the worries that have gone through my head on an endless loop for the past twenty-four hours. I needed a mental break to ground myself so I could focus and think clearly about my next moves.

I'm not certain if this mansion is someone's permanent residence or if it's always this decked out for impromptu parties—I expect that a few members have more than one residence here—but it's beautiful and haunting all at once, like a spectacular crystal chandelier covered with the dust and spider webs of neglect. Part classical mansion, part creepy fantasy, the aesthetic brings to mind haunted houses and palaces where ghosts would cavort with Gods of old. Shakespeare would have given his eyeteeth to have lived in a place such as this, and to have had his muse tickled by the decor.

Stairs that lead to the ceiling. Doors that open into random rooms that are impractically small. Bookcases that are ladders leading to new rooms. It's more like Acid in Wonderland meets M.C. Escher. Maybe that's redundant; I can't decide. I'm having a hard time pegging exactly what the house's motif is—which is probably the exact thing the host was going for. They likely care more about the guests anyways.

One thing is for sure, the guests have gone all out when it comes to their costume choices—and the execution thereof. There are no duds among us.

Near a fountain made of mermaids in reverse—the legs and shapely asses of women and the heads of fish—there's a guy painted up like Michelangelo's David, but instead of a penis, there's a bright green apple dangling between his legs, no doubt meant to represent the original sin. I wonder if there's an Eve around here who came as his date.

Standing by the bar is a woman whose gown is a melted clock, dripping time, with her face painted up as a pretty skull, and even though it doesn't quite fit the motif, it works. She's speaking to a man with a tiny top hat and a suit that's too small, wearing the mask of a baby, so he looks like a giant infant in fancy dress. The effect is unnerving, for sure.

A woman in a fancy tuxedo with a fuzzy moth's head and antenna leans against the mantelpiece, talking to a man with a scorpion for a head.

There's the ubiquitous rabbit and horse head masks, ornate and stiff affairs that must make the wearers sweat like crazy beneath them, but they must not mind since they're on the dance floor, shaking their asses like the drunk uncle at a wedding.

The music is interesting, and creepy, and it takes me a moment to realize that it's the Beatles being played backwards over Wagner, but there's an underlying bassline tying them together into something that curiously works.

A woman walks around with a frame over an ornate skirt, but instead of fabric there are hundreds of glasses of champagne and wine in metal holders. An interesting way of serving us while ignoring us as she sedately strolls around, taking her skirt for a walk, almost as though she's not at the party, but at the house in another time where it's not filled with guests and sounds and life.

A lady's got on a blonde wig to go with her plain black dress, and I'm disappointed that she hasn't even tried. Then she turns and I see that she's painted her face exactly as Dali's painting, *Mae West's Face Which May Be Used As A Surrealist Apartment*, complete with tiny wooden picture frames around her eyes, and I smile at her. She nods and turns back to her conversation with a man who's got a lobster claw as a hand and a cage over his head and shoulders. Impractical, but interesting.

As I head deeper into the house, the clothes get skimpier and people are engaging in obviously sexual activities. A woman with a hat that looks like three sets of hands caressing her face, but their nails look more like eagle talons and leave indentations in her skin. Her black cat suit has the breasts and crotch cut out, and a man in a tight black leotard with one of those creepy plague masks over his penis sucks on one of her nipples. He's clearly embellishing the size of his penis with that mask, but it makes me smile as well.

A woman is painted up to look like the keys of a piano with giant gorilla hands "playing" her breasts and vagina to cover them, but she's on her knees in front of a woman, lifting up her filthy potato sack loincloth and going to town licking her pussy. The woman receiving her attention is painted completely blue with gemstones, probably real, over her features, making a mask of wealth, to go with the plain potato sack clothes.

I'm not sure if they came together, pun intended, but if their costumes have a complementary theme, I'm not getting it. Something deep and dramatic about wealth and taste, or culture and waste? Then again, I went with something easy to pull off that would still fit in on short notice. Maybe they did exactly the same.

Inside another room, this one with strange foam geometric shapes as furniture, I see a man in a black corset and fishnet stockings with a bowler hat over of his flawless bob. His moustache is perfectly coiffed and doesn't move at all as another man with a perfectly tailored suit, normal except for his upside down moustache—and the way two large fish are swallowing his feet, all the way up to his knees—fucks him from behind with brutal thrusts.

Huh. This must be the orgy room of the house, as nearly everyone in it has a hand or a mouth full of someone else.

It makes me feel like skipping, but I head through another door. No sense settling for door number one before I get to see what's behind doors two and three, right?

The next room is less surreal but has a more nautical theme, and is about ten degrees colder, maybe meant to represent the ocean?

A woman with a mermaid tail and tiny dragon wings, her hair a wig made of coins that look like fish scales and tinkle when she moves, lies on a bench seat near a wall. I wonder if she's mobile, or if she's stuck in that spot for the duration unless someone carries her wherever she wants to go, like a maharaja.

A man in brown satin lederhosen with two large white dildos as walrus tusks rubs the fake teeth against the crotch of a woman, naked except for a mask like a giant, blue seahorse.

I slip through a small door I notice behind a curtain, the door-jamb just peeking through it as though it's more private and whoever is inside doesn't quite want to be noticed or joined.

Inside a completely black room, men and women in black and white cavort beneath a black light, nothing showing up except the white bits that glow so bright they almost hurt my eyes. I'm not sure if the fluids on their skins are paint or bodily fluids, actually, but they rub up against each other and writhe on the floor, spreading liquid light wherever they touch.

I skirt the edge of the room, interested in the ocean of bodies moving together, but not drawn to it enough to make this where I want to spend the rest of my night.

I pass through a thick curtain and walk down a hallway into an S&M club I'd expect to see in a Gaspar Noe film. Now this is more like it. A large fountain in the middle of the room is the only sound, other than the slaps of crops and whips against skin.

I stick out like a surreal thumb, the only one not dressed in strappy leather and vinyl numbers, but I don't mind. We aren't in a Berlin sex club; the rules are different here. I take a seat at a table in the corner, intent on observing before joining in. What do I feel like tonight? The tall woman, built like an Amazon? The slender man, barely more than a boy? The elegant older woman with corkscrew curls? Dominant, submissive…switch?

I turn toward a small glimmer of light that catches my eye from a few feet away. A mirror. I move my hand to fix my hair and realize it's not a mirror but a window.

*I think we have a winner.*

I head towards it, certain that this is where I'm meant to be tonight.

I shimmy past a table where two muscled men, Dominants, are fucking a man, mouth and ass. His black lipstick is smeared all over his face, but his eyes roll back in his head as the man at his ass hits the spot.

The window swings forward, part of a well-concealed door, and I step inside even though it's dark and I can't see the room nor its inhabitants.

It clicks closed behind me when I take a few steps inside.

The lights come up slowly, theatrically, and I blink and turn to see whose hand is on the dimmer switch.

My skin crawls.

Mr. X. But of course.

The bastard smiles, smugly, and it occurs to me that I should have asked whose party this was before attending. It's embarrassing how rookie of a mistake this was and I should have known, especially after the conference, that he'd be waiting for one last chance to intimidate me. Well, if this is another of his attempts to scare me, it's still not going to happen—though I have decided on a gentler approach: the good old, "tell them what they want to hear, then do exactly as you want." Sort of like how it's easier to ask for forgiveness instead of permission, only I'm not going to ask for either.

It's not as though I have any real dirt on him, so I don't know what his preoccupation with my article is about. He's the one who put me onto it, for fuck's sake.

"Mr. X. I should have known this was your party."

"You really should have," he practically purrs, happy I'm in his trap. "Who else could throw a party the way I can?"

I incline my head, unable to argue with the quality I've seen tonight, though my instincts keep telling me to run far and fast from this room. Privacy is not my friend when it comes to this man. "Interesting theme, though it isn't carried all through the house. Are your parties always like this?"

"You tell me." His gaze narrows and he takes a step closer.

"What are you talking about?"

"Do you remember when we first met?"

"Yes, it was—"

"No. It wasn't. The first time I saw you, you were being set on a chair by a man in a mask. I'd seen you wandering through the mansion that night at my party, and thought nothing of you...until you came to life, ravenous for cock as though you lived on come. That's when I first saw you."

If he saw that, then that means—

"I knew I was right to film you that night. I had no idea our paths would cross again, but you made a name for yourself, and I heard you come up in certain circles. Naturally, I grew curious as to what you'd gotten up to in the years that had passed since last I'd seen your face."

My heart stutters in my chest at his confession. "You were willing to ruin my career just to get me to come here. You knew I'd do anything to prove myself after the scandal...the one you caused."

He wiggles his eyebrows as though we're sharing a delightful joke.

Clearly, he doesn't care that I know everything. Why is he telling me this? Why now? And yet, I should have known it was him from the beginning. "My wealthy benefactor, giving me leads on stories. Why? We'd never met before, you owed me nothing. Was it just about power, so you could pretend that you're the reason I have a career—

which is ridiculous, by the way. You can't undercut my accomplishments. Or was this your plan all along—to get me to write what you wanted to give yourself a thin veneer of morality to whomever you were trying to impress? Only, that's the part I don't understand in all of this. Why use me and not someone else who actually gives a damn or is on your payroll? We didn't even know each other before your little friend Dominick gave me your message."

"Dominick was hired for a purpose. I wouldn't call us friends." He grins. "Oh, you and I had met before that, Catherine. It's been a while and you were a little out of it that night, so I'm not surprised your memories of me are hazy."

"I have no memories of you at all." I grit my teeth at the smugness in his voice. "Whatever you think you saw the night we allegedly met—"

"Oh, we more than met, my darling. It piqued my interest to see you again and to be perfectly honest, I liked knowing I'd had my hands in your cunt, that you'd gotten me off, and you hadn't known it was me, hadn't known we'd been close enough for me to come on you. You chatted about the most banal shit, trying to present yourself as a young professional career woman when all along I knew what a little cock gobbler you truly are. Do you know, sometimes we'd be texting, and I'd be watching the video of you sucking my cock?" He laughs and shakes his head. "Of course you didn't know that. Well, you know now. Doesn't that feel good? I certainly feel as though a weight has been lifted. The truth shall set you free!"

I suppress a shudder at the things he's saying and the implications of his confession. Conversations I'd thought innocent suddenly take on a more sinister air. He was never a friend or colleague. He was a predator, and the thought of him talking to me, the knowledge that he got into my apartment, laid out a dress—that I actually wore— and watched me that night after the interview chills me. Not that I'll let him know that. I cock a hip and feign nonchalance I definitely don't feel.

This is a man I need to tread carefully around. He's deranged and dangerous and not above…anything. And yet, I refuse to show any fear to let him think he's gotten to me. "So what, I jerked a lot of people off that night. Your dick wasn't anything special."

He shrugs. "You're a whore."

"And you want to fuck me. That's it, isn't it?" I step closer, noting his chest heaving, the way he squirms on his feet, turned on. "You were mad that DeVille was the one who got to fuck me and you didn't. Is that why it had to be me all along? Revenge against Bob? Revenge against me not magically remembering you when I heard your voice? When you saw me in the dress, did you jerk off, wishing you could touch my skin like it was touching me? Did you curse Dominick for getting to stick his cock inside me, to lick my asshole and eat me out? To be the one on top of me?" Something dawns on me and I change tactics. "To be the one underneath me?"

His pupils dilate and I smile. "I've got to say, X, that this long game you were going for is impressive. You were willing to build me up so I'd crash so hard that nothing would survive that fall. You were willing to fuck up my life to get what you wanted."

"I was," he hisses.

I lick my lips, noticing the bondage gear in the room. "And what is it you truly want?"

"You know what I want, Catherine."

I smile. "Well, guess what? Tonight's your lucky night. You're finally going to get fucked."

He grins as I grab his wrists and haul him to the bench, pushing him down onto it with a thud. I straddle him and reach above his head to a table while he runs his hands over my hips and ass, hard, greedily like a little inexperienced boy.

I put the big, red ball gag I grab from the table in his mouth, tying the straps behind his head, hard, and kiss the ball like it's his mouth. His lids get heavy and I can feel his cock swelling against me. Now my heart starts to pound.

Men who crave power feel their most vulnerable when you take it away from them.

I want him to know how that feels.

I stand and strip him from the waist down then guide him to turn around, surprised when he goes with it. He must think I'm going to spank him, like I have some kind of interest in his salt and pepper pubes and twisted little rat brain.

I use the restraints on the bench to cuff his wrists above his head. The bench isn't just a bench—it's got handy hydraulics that lift one end up, so his toes barely touch the floor and his hands are stretched above his head. Mr. X spares no expense with his kink. I eschew the ankle cuffs—they've got too much give for what I have in mind, so I turn him around and fasten a spreader bar in between his ankles before locking them into place with the metal rings on the bottom of the bench. Perfect for what I've got in mind for him.

I walk around to look him in the eyes and smile, crouching in front of him so we're eye to eye. "You're a pathetic piece of shit. Whatever power you've managed to buy for yourself with your daddy's money has rotted your mind. Men like you have to buy people, or bribe them into being with you because at the core of it all, you're weak little nothings. There's no heart, no soul, nothing interesting or creative to be drawn to. All you are is a bank account and"—I look down between us—"a disappointing cock. No wonder I didn't remember you. You're utterly forgettable."

He squirms hard, but that's the glorious thing about bondage. I pat the gag he's chomping on, trying to talk around to no avail. "Shh. You'll hurt yourself, flailing around like that. You've done enough talking. My turn. Listen carefully, X. See, I'm not the sweet young thing I was back when we first met. I'm not even the same woman I was last week. I've learned so much and had time to cram a few aces up my sleeve. You'd do well to remember that before threatening me again. You have no idea what I'm capable of, and I'll write whatever the fuck I want."

I stand, but the flicker of scorn in his eyes irritates me to the point of fury. He doesn't think I can do anything to him. Here is a man who truly believes he is untouchable. This man has burned my life to the ground for nothing more than sport, and killed people I loved. Who else could have killed Inana and Anna? What other skeletons are in his closet?

I peruse the other items on the table, selecting and sliding a black cloth mask over his face—the type kidnappers use that completely cover their victims' heads.

I tighten the ribbon a little too tightly around his neck, glorying in the way he thrashes harder and makes little gagging sounds. "You're pathetic. You with your cartoon villain name, trying to garner an air of mystery. But for all of your riches, when it comes down to it, you are just as fragile as any of us are."

I imagine tightening the ribbon even more until he stops breathing and moving completely. I'm sure no one would kick up too much a fuss over this waste of skin.

But no matter what we can get away with when no one's looking and our friends can cover the truth, we still have to look ourselves in the mirror every day. And as much as I hate this man, I let go of the ribbon. His breathing slowly returns to normal inside the bag, though he's still bound, gagged, and stuck in the fabric.

"I'm better than you are, X. I could do the most evil things to you and not feel bad because of the way you care so little for those around you." But I refuse to kill him. That would make me just as bad as he is.

I head back out of the room to the little table with the Dominants and whisper in their ears, giving them a gift.

An open door, a huge tube of lube, and a man who wanted to be fucked by a few anonymous strangers all night long.

Hard.

They promise to oblige and take very good care of my slave.

I walk out of the room, leaving him with his ass in the air and his legs spread, waiting for the two men he doesn't know are coming.

What a perfect party.

*That's for Anna and Inana.*

*That's for my life you tried to take as well.*

# TWENTY-THREE

∿∿∿

A WHITE, HORSE-DRAWN CARRIAGE pulls up to my house and I climb onto it, careful not to get the hem of my gown caught in the wheels. The dress twinkles in the light, brilliant gemstones reflecting back the sun and sending prisms out from where I stand.

I sit and the driver, decked out in a plum tuxedo and top hat, moves us forward down the road with a flick of the reins. The horses' hooves clack against the road, marking the time of our journey, only I can't quite remember where it is we're meant to be going. Am I late for something, or years too early?

I've left my gloves at home, and I dig inside my small clutch to see if I brought a spare pair. I did not. I open my mouth to tell the driver to halt and turn around, but a shimmering cloud on the road ahead draws my attention. It's pretty and the air seems to hum the closer we get to it.

I reach my hand over the side of the carriage as we touch the cloud. But it's not glitter, or sparkles. Not magical at all. It's a swarm of bugs. So many mosquitoes.

I'm covered by them from head to toe. I open my mouth to tell the driver to go back, but they fill my mouth, biting my tongue as well.

Every inch of my skin is coated with the tiny pricks of pain as they stab into me and feed. My hand itches, worse than anywhere else, and I scratch at it, flinching when it comes back wet. I look down, surprised at all the blood. Where is it coming from?

I dig with my fingers, trying to move the redness aside so I can find where the injury is, but it's too thick. And yet, I can't find a puncture wound or a cut. I look around to see if it's been dripped onto me, but it's as though it's seeping through my skin through a million tiny bites.

I can't stop it—there's no way I can keep my blood in my body when every inch of me is squeezing the vital fluid from my body through the pores of my skin and I'm terrified but the carriage goes forward at its sedate pace, a contrast to my growing panic.

I grab my gown and wrap the top of it over my head like a hood, trying to use it as a tourniquet or a shield for my arms and face, now dripping with blood as well. But the fabric starts billowing like there's too much of it, or the dress is growing, or I'm shrinking, and I fall, drowning in fabric and blood and it's so hard to breathe.

I wake up tangled in the sheets, my sweat coating me in the sheen I'd mistaken for blood in my sleep. I forgot to turn the air conditioning on before getting into bed.

I kick the covers off, get a glass of water, and strip my soaking tank top and panties off before slipping back into bed.

It's only the female mosquitoes that feed off of blood. They also feed on nectar and water like the males, but need the iron and the protein found in blood for their eggs. They feed from us to create life. This inelegance of nature, the raw savagery of it makes me wonder how people can call it intelligently designed…and yet, the fragility of it all seems to give credence to that. You take one thing out and so much falls apart like a house of cards.

It's why I don't think humans will last forever. We're much too destructive. L.A. looks like a weird growth, a tumor on the landscape belching smog into the air, killing any natural beauty. We're not supposed to be there—there's no natural means of life in a place that hot. But because we arrogantly decide that man trumps nature, we savage the areas nature tells us we shouldn't be. We ignore the earthquakes and tsunamis and weather that kills. We ignore predators and poisonous things and a dearth of natural resources, shipping them in as needed which creates even more pollution.

Still, it's as though people have forgotten that man is a part of nature, not above it or separate from it. We're not even at the top of the food chain if you take away our weapons and tools and technology. Send a few humans onto a reality show where they're on a deserted island, and it's barely a day and some are breaking down sobbing that they miss their families, jumping at every bump in the night. We're not built for the elements—we've created things that block nature from ourselves as much as possible.

We move to ridiculously hot places with no natural water supplies and crank the air conditioning until we shiver and need to put on sweaters.

We move to incredibly cold places with no food sources and wait for winter so we can truck supplies into them on roads made of ice.

We do everything we can to get rid of nature—hell, even tearing up yards and replacing them with rocks, and then we pack up the family into a shitty little RV and go camping on the weekends in the summertime, breathing in the fresh air for a day to remind ourselves how fortunate we are to be able to get away from it all when everyone's on a treadmill of consumerism.

You want a motorbike so you can feel like a rebel and to be free, but then you get a giant one with all the bells and whistles so it basically looks like you're riding a couch down the road. Perhaps this drive to accumulate is part of our evolution. It's not unique to our species—think of that parable of the ant and the grasshopper. Live in the now or worry about the future—there will always be people who ascribe to both ways of life. We want to have and keep and glut and that's okay. It's part of our natures to want the things that we perceive as making us happy. At the end of the day, we're all going to take that dirt nap. It's unavoidable, inescapable. It's life. It's death. Balance.

Nature is a deadly thing, but beautiful as well, always seeking the balance we're avoiding by thinking we know better.

When you think about it, in nature, it tends to be the females of the species that are the most deadly. If the males don't get devoured after sex (praying mantis, most spiders) they end up with their penises snapped off and they bleed to death (bees). Lionesses are the ones who hunt—and there's nothing deadlier than a mama bear defending her cubs.

Humans seem to be the only ones who have gone against their nature, cultivating women into pretty things, softened for men's pleasure. We become yielding and dreamy, fantasies for them to sink their hard cocks into. The warrior women are only attractive when the men think of taming them. Few like the ball busting career woman who gets shit done. If they want to fuck her, it's to see the transformation they've created. They want her hair to come out of that tight bun, the glasses to come off and reveal her beautiful doe eyes.

It's about the chase and the challenge and as soon as it's attained, it's boring. It's familiar. Safe sex is dangerous for relationships. Safe sex—by that, I mean the safety of predictability—kills. Routine kills. We let them chase us, paint our lips and faces, wear heels to make the view better for them as we prance away, a challenge to their evolutionary traits of capture and conquer.

We let people bleed the life from us, spending hours on things that don't matter because we think we're supposed to want that connection with someone else. We teach people to be ashamed if they can fuck someone without growing attached and wanting to breed with them. We mince and prance and shame others instead of taking long hard looks at ourselves and owning our choices.

I did something tonight that I never would have thought was a part of my nature, if you'd asked me a week ago, a year ago, ten. What else has changed within the depths of myself? If faced with other situations, how would I react? Can I count on the reactions I'd expect of myself, or is a new version of me being born in the dark corners of my subconscious mind?

If eyes are a window to the soul, then the subconscious is a window into our minds, and dreams are the key to it all.

Dreams have always fascinated me. I stretch out in the dark, remembering one recurring dream I had as a child. It was always the same; I was standing on a railway track on a sunny day. I wore a bright green dress that I didn't own in real life, but it was my favorite in the dream. I think it was what one of the characters from one of my favorite television shows always wore.

There were bright sunflowers on the sides of the tracks, just outside of the rails, and I was trying to reach one more, even though my arms were already filled. I was trying to get them so I could give them to the birds to eat, and my little arms were hugging the long stalks as the heads obscured my vision.

I remember the crunch of the gravel beneath my little feet as I hopped from plank to plank heading to give the birds their treat that I'd painstakingly gathered. I always looked over my shoulder for a train, but none ever came and I was never truly worried one would come. Now, I'd be looking over my shoulder the whole time, panicky that a train was bearing down on me with a rumbling I could feel in my bones. But then, it was idyllic and peaceful and hazy around the edges in the way that only truly perfect moments can be, even if they're just dreams.

Except for the way my teeth were crumbling out of my head, which apparently symbolizes regret or embarrassment, but I don't know why I'd have felt that way at such a young age. Maybe it was that I was sick of my actual baby teeth falling out and leaving gaps that made me lisp, and it was bleeding into my subconscious because I hated it so much. But I'd carefully spit out the tooth fragments as they came loose, trying very hard not to swallow them. I've had dreams with teeth coming out that as an adult have been disconcerting.

Maybe children don't see danger where they should, or feel regret like they learn to.

The subconscious mind is like the depths of the ocean. Things are always happening down there that we don't know about. Things that form and shape us, for better or worse. Tiny ripples leading to big waves. Maybe I should feel bad about Mr. X.

But it's funny, the things you can do to someone and not regret a tiny bit.

Does that make me a bad person? I'm not sure. The older I get, the more I learn of the world, the grayer words like "good" and "bad" become. What's the difference between vengeance and revenge? Retribution and justice? Where's the line when avenging someone goes too far and tips over into turning the hero into an anti-hero?

I take Inana's diary to bed with me, stroking the cover as though it's a pet, a familiar. My lover's hand. I can't bring her back, but right now I feel like if she were here, she'd be happy with what I did, calling it poetic justice for a man who gives so little thought to fucking others over.

# TWENTY-FOUR

*ళిஇ஡ℓ*

SOME DAYS YOU WAKE UP alert but peaceful, as though a veil has been slowly pulled from your eyes and mind. The lighting feels different. Your body feels different, as though every position is comfortable when if you tried lying that way at any other time, it would be terrible. You're content to lie in bed and think about everything and nothing, maybe try to remember your dream and analyze it.

I wake up in the morning like that and reach for the diary.

Inana's diary is gone, but Anna is sitting on the bed beside me like she's been gently waiting for me to wake up for hours, and all I can think is that the shade of gray her camisole is makes her skin seem extra peachy. It's inane and I want to laugh but I'm afraid to even breathe.

Anna. My Achilles heel, the fatal blonde who I'd have followed to the ends of the earth. I just never knew that's what I was doing. I didn't know she was still alive and I didn't know until this moment, seeing her now, that in my heart of hearts, I'd truly thought she was dead. My breath feels thick and hot, my throat constricting with emotion.

My journey was one Anna set me on, and now that I'm in deeper than I could ever have imagined diving, here she is, as if pulled from my dreams.

"I thought you were dead."

Her eyes squeeze shut for a moment before she gives me eye contact again. "I am," she whispers.

I reach out, tentatively, and caress her face. Solid, warm, real. She presses against my hand, cupping it with both of hers to nuzzle into my touch.

I sit up and I slip my fingertips down to her neck, gently pushing against the artery pumping beneath her skin. For someone who's dead, her pulse is steady and strong.

"Figuratively," I say accusatorily. "How could you let me think you were dead?" I tear my hand away when all I want is to pull her close and squeeze her tightly to prove she's here and real and okay.

I stand and pace, not looking away from her the whole time, but unable to sit still with this, this, *everything* coursing through me. "Did you know that I mourned you? Did you know that I buried you in my mind just so I could move on and keep breathing? Did you know that for a while I doubted that you'd actually even existed, or if you were some delusion my subconscious had dreamed up?" Like Fight Club, but with fucking, for she'd led me directly into this crazy Fuck Club that was The Juliette Society, then left me in it to drown in decadence all by myself.

She gave me the noose to hang myself with, and now here I am in a compound with a man who probably wants me dead, depending on what I choose to do, what I choose to write.

"I've missed you," she whispers.

I crash into her, pulling her close, crushing her curves against mine in a hug I can't make tight enough. My arms haven't got the strength to convince me she's safe and here.

And I wasn't intending on making this sexual, but somehow my teeth find her neck and clamp down and she stiffens and my tongue shoots out to feel her skin, to taste her as well, because I can smell her and feel her and taste her and see her, but I still can't believe she's real.

But she moans and yields against me, softening beneath my touch. My fingers strip her of her clothes with nimble movements that make it seem like I've done this a thousand times before, or practiced, or maybe just dreamed of doing it.

I have.

And then we're both naked, nothing but flesh and desire and relief and hunger.

She's still curvy but her collarbones jut out a little more sharply than I remember, her shoulders a bit bonier beneath my roving hands.

She reacts to me like a cat, leaning into my caresses and practically purring, eyes closing as her breathing increases. I lead her to the bed and guide her to her back, climbing on top of her, framing her face with my forearms, bracing myself above her.

Her lips are full and softer than I imagined they'd be beneath mine. I arch my back and trace her nipples with mine, shivering at the simple pleasure of the silky sensation of her skin on mine.

We were always the same. Shapeable, moldable. And yet different. A still, calm, pool of water—and a crashing ocean.

I'm just not sure who was who.

But we belonged at each other's side, supporting and caring. Bolstering the other, filling in the gaps where courage flagged. But somehow we did it apart. She got here and so did I. Our different journeys led us to the same destination like it was fate.

I slide a hand down her body and grab her hip before trailing it between her legs and delving inside the wetness I find there, rubbing it viciously over her clit.

She cries out, and as she moans my name, I swallow it, licking it from her lips, nipping at them as a gentle punishment for leaving me to pick up the pieces.

I don't forgive her.

I never forgot her.

I'll always forgive her.

*Eventually.*

I coat her lips with the wetness from my finger, my belly tightening when she licks it off while staring deep into my eyes. Aligning our clits, I rock my hips, setting a fast rhythm, not caring if she wants me to go faster or slower. This is what it is, it is what we are now that she left and I became this version of myself.

I kiss her, tasting her lips and pussy, and plunge my tongue deep in her mouth, claiming hers with mine before pulling back to look at her face.

She takes what I give her with that same smile, and soon I'm fucking her in earnest and tomorrow I'll have bruises on my pussy but right now I don't care, and my juices drip down to mingle with hers and it makes us slide around and around, and it smells like sex and sweetness and increases the heat with it but I'd set us both on fire with the friction of my hips before stopping now.

Her nails rake my back and she pulls me closer and the sharp points she digs in anchor me and suddenly I'm coming and coming with deep gasps that fill my lungs and make my hands clench around sections of her hair. Pulling them makes her shake and she cries out with the pain, coming with me.

I bury my face in her neck and let her gently trace my back with her fingertips, just breathing in the scent of her flesh and our sex.

Words elude me.

I want to do it again, more thoroughly, this time with her tied up in my playroom and giving me the answers I seek.

But I don't need whips and chains and vibrators to get answers.

She owes me an explanation.

The whole thing has a surreal edge to it and I'm suddenly afraid I never woke up at all and this is just another dream, crueler than the last.

But when I pull back, she smiles, and the guilt in her eyes solidifies reality again. I know she's truly here, for dream versions of those who wrong us feel no guilt when they wound us deeply enough to leave scars on who we are.

"I can't believe you're finally here," she whispers.

Her whispers worry me. They're so unlike the boisterous woman I knew who used to say the most outlandish thing.

There are dark circles beneath her eyes as well.

"Why are you here, Anna?" I get off her and wrap the blanket around me, leaving her the sheet. "It's been years. You could have gotten in touch at any time."

"I couldn't." She sits up, moving to rest against the headboard. "It's complicated."

"Tell me the truth. You owe me that at least." I missed her so damn much, but with the orgasm and initial shock of her appearance wearing off, I want some answers. "I deserve some answers."

"And you'll get them."

The man's voice that says that comes from the door to the bedroom.

# TWENTY-FIVE

~oᗯᗝᗝᗯ~

DOMINICK STANDS AT THE OPEN DOOR but doesn't come in.

I stiffen at the sight of Mr. X's lapdog. Whom I willingly fucked on more than one occasion. "What the hell are you doing here?"

Anna sees who it is and puts a hand on my arm. "Catherine, he's with me, with us."

I shake her hand off me. "Is that what he told you? Because X had a different side of the story." I cross my arms, feeling betrayed when she doesn't seem surprised by my words.

Dominick doesn't move from by the door. "X thinks I work solely for him but I've been a double agent, so to speak. The car accident was me, too—attempting to extract you safely when we realized what Mr. X was planning for you."

Admitting he begged or bribed someone to crash into me on purpose does nothing to endear himself to me. I could have been injured more seriously than I was—they're called accidents for a reason. There's only so much you can plan when it comes to something like that. The situation was not under control. Shards of glass, innocent bystanders, as it was I ended up banged up pretty badly. Too much could have gone wrong, and it gives me chills. And yet, his words penetrate the anger. "Extract me?" I turn back to Anna, wondering if she'd have fucked me if not for her agenda, whatever it is.

"Get you out. Not just the car, or the situation with him. We were going to save you by bringing you here. What happened to Inana almost happened to me."

She's being deliberately vague, but why? I remember Anna telling me she had a boyfriend, this one guy, who liked to treat her rough and leave his mark for others to know where he'd been. And that was fine with her too. *"I love to feel them on my body,"* she'd said. *"As long as I can see them and feel them, I remember how they got there. I remember how he put his hands on me. How he fucked me. And I like to watch them fade. From red to black to green to gold. And when they fade away to nothing, I know it's time to hook up with him again."*

I narrow my eyes at her, remembering her words, parroting them back to her now. "Out of all your boyfriends, you thought you liked him the best of all, because he was the only one who thought the way that you did. Who believed that 'sex and violence are two sides of the same coin.' Who not only believed it, but acted upon it." Janus. Right there the whole time.

Her nod affirms it.

"That was X, wasn't it? The one who used to mark you up?" I ask, not adding about how she was scared of him because I already know the answer.

She rubs her arms to get rid of the goosebumps I can see even from here.

"He thought he'd killed me. He went way too far in a scene and the faction stepped in, seeing their opportunity when he left me for dead and called them to 'take care of me,' the same way he'd done with Inana Luna."

Despite the horror of the situation and the story she's telling me, hearing that name on Anna's lips sends a thrill through my spine and down my limbs. "He killed her?"

"He maintains that it was an accident. That the scene got out of control, but it's difficult to believe him, with his history." She continues. "I loved your story about her, by the way. It was as if you knew her. You perfectly captured her." She shakes her head to clear it. "I've been living in JS safe houses, bouncing from place to place, first recovering then finding somewhere that's more permanent while also gathering intel on him."

"And yet you've ended up here on the island right under his nose?"

She nods. "Dominick and I are part of a faction. They're the ones who have kept me safe after making me disappear."

"And you wanted to do the same to me. This faction? What is it you do?"

Dominick's voice comes from much closer this time. "He's not someone who can be told what to do. We believe the only way to neutralize him is from an outside source. This isn't just about him or us. Think of us as the cleanup crew. We step in when things get messy and put them to right. Unfortunately, he has gone over the line on more than one occasion."

"And was planning something similar with me?" I ask, now feeling more than a little glad about the way I left his crazy ass, though I wish I'd have taken the lube with me when I left him there with the Doms.

Anna shakes her head. "He's not like that. With him, it's more a case of spontaneously going too far, past the point of no return. It would be an accident, but the result would be the same." Her gaze clouds. "He's vicious when he wants to be and we saw how things were progressing."

I want to know exactly what he did to her so I can do it to him, but revenge isn't what they need me for. "And I got on his bad side by not doing as I was told like a good little girl. And now you think he was about to cross the line again so you're here first, exposing yourselves and telling me the truth about your disappearance. To prepare me for what's coming next." I understand. They mean fake my death just as they'd faked Anna's to get her out of his radar. "Would he have even believed the same thing had happened a second time? Actually a third, because of Inana."

Anna shrugs. "Even if he didn't believe in his shitty luck with potential partners, he feels things so shallowly he'd have found another toy soon enough. And if he had cared enough to notice you'd gone missing after the accident, he'd have assumed it was an enemy taking out someone he wanted in order to annoy him."

Murder as means of annoyance. It's not hard to see how a man like this would have terrible enemies as well. I knew this was a dangerous man, but I had no idea how close I'd come to being snuffed out. "And why are you telling me now instead of staying in the shadows, scuttling around and pulling strings in the dark?"

Anna's full lips thin into a tight line. "It's not like that, Catherine. I can't even count the amount of times I wanted to call you, text you, or try to communicate with you, but he'd have traced it and found me, no matter how carefully I'd hidden the truth in code, risking everything my friends had done for me." She looks at Dominick and smiles before turning back to me with a more somber expression. "And then, when it finally was safe to send you, I don't know, a letter or anything—by that time, he'd set his sights on you instead. Moved on to you, and again I couldn't risk it for selfish reasons."

Selfish reasons. Are there any other kinds? I let her words sink in. I'm in this mess because of her. Directly and indirectly, for if I'd never met her, I wouldn't have been drawn in. I should be furious, but I can't gather enough outrage to be truly angry at her. I can't even get mad at Dominick for leading me down the garden path, as they say, even though he fucked me. I asked him to and definitely can't regret those nights.

I turn to him as something else occurs to me. "Your video at the industry party. That was this place, meant to lure me in, wasn't it?"

He nods. "And you almost blew it for me when you asked him about Honduras. I had a lot of explaining to do to him that night."

How much of my life have they directed over these past few years? Can I be mad at those who have given me so much, taken so much? Not with everything I've seen and learned. Not with the way it's all shaped me into something I've grown to like.

Dominick fills the silence I leave. "We're outing themselves because you had no idea how close you came to being killed by X—and you need to keep your distance from him...but there's also the matter of exposing him. We were days away from getting you out. We'd have manipulated the crash so he'd have thought you'd passed away from injuries sustained there. But the next day he released the video of you. . . . We didn't foresee that, unfortunately."

"Yes, it sure was unfortunate how you failed to stop one of your own members from burning my reputation and career to the ground. Try completely fucked up and irresponsible... and for nothing." I shake my head, remembering waking up in cold bathwater. I could have died then. "You trashed my car and put me at risk for nothing."

Anna sits straighter. "That's just it. We didn't go through with the plan because there's still a way we can turn this around. But we needed the notoriety he'd created around you to do it."

Dominick nods. "The faction we're a part of believes that now is the time to take him down. He's gotten out of control, growing more reckless by the day. More people are going to die, and he's also risking exposing us."

I bark out a laugh, truly amused at the way he's trying to appeal to my emotions right now. "Why should I care about a few members of a society who didn't give a damn about me—especially if I was in so much danger. This place is responsible for breeding a man like this and allowing him to thrive. Why didn't they redirect him to someone else, or step in and tell him to stop? Surely there's someone who could force him." I shake my head. "No, you know what I think? It seems like you're trying to scare me into doing your dirty work—

because it would be dirty. If he was so close to losing control when he thought there was a possibility I'd write something he didn't want, it's going to be nuclear if I actually go against him." My skin heats up with passion. "Why should I? Why should I risk being killed for any of you?"

"Because it's not just about us and The Juliette Society anymore. This is massive, bigger than any of us could have dreamed, Catherine." Anna's words come out fast, hushed, urgently. "You've heard of the Zika Virus?"

"Of course I have." I haven't been living under a rock.

Dominick sets a dossier of info on the bed, including the USB.

Yeah, that one. The same one they'd taken from me after La Notte. I'm struck with a prescient feeling that hits me like an internal earthquake. Because if this is, in fact, the same USB, then I could have done something to stop X four fucking years ago. "Is this the one you took away from me when I chose to tell Inana's story?"

He nods.

If they were giving me the chance to take X down then and I turned it down to tell Inana's story, that means that in a way, everything he's done for the past four years has partially been down to me. It's like that old proverb: If you save a man's life, you become responsible for him.

Because I didn't take him down then, he's been going around taking lives, unchecked. Then again, there were at least a few people in The Juliette Society who knew what he was up to the whole time. My sense of guilt lessens marginally when I realize they've also known about this information, whatever it is, for longer than me, and chose to sit on it. "You're giving me another shot at this?"

Dominick nods. "There's always been a darker side of The Juliette Society. Naturally, when you have certain people involved in it, people who are accustomed to having power and prestige get it by nefarious means. Not all, but enough to abuse the privilege they've attained. Our faction wants things to be blown open because dark things live in the shadows of power. It needs to be transparent once inside or we'll rot from within."

"I can understand that. But what's that got to do with Zika?"

Dominick plunges ahead. "X is very into designer viruses that help with 'population control,' as he's into Eugenics. You're familiar with Eugenics?"

"Hitler and his bullshit 'superior race,' right?"

He nods. "Selective breeding, yes, to encourage positive traits you want to propagate, but it's also about weeding out the ones you wish to end to discourage negative traits from continuing. Some people already do it in society in less controversial or malicious ways."
He gives me a moment to let this sink in, but he doesn't need to.

"He's using it for population control in places like Honduras. Places where there aren't as many vaccine programs and health care options."

Dominick nods.

Zika can cause paralysis and cause birth defects as well, the worst in my opinion being microcephaly. I remember seeing videos of babies who'd been born with the virus. My heart broke for the babies affected, and their families, for their lives had changed as well because of their baby's needs.

And yet it seems diametrically opposite to his idea of a better, healthier future. He's creating illness instead of curing it. He's using Zika as population control in areas of the world he deems unworthy of living.

This is too big. We've all idly or actively wished for the end of cancer, a cure for AIDS. We've all sat and toasted to world peace, and cringed at the news when another report of violence or a pandemic comes to the forefront. In the moment we'd do anything to see it stopped, give anything for our world to be a better place not only for ourselves, but for the generations to come.

But this is too big for me to take in. A band of pressure forms over the top of my head as my shoulders solidify with tension. We're not talking about a throwaway decision here, and the weight of Anna's and Dominick's stares and hopes is too much pressure. I can't breathe. "I need you two to leave."

Anna shakes her head. "Catherine—"

"I need to think! Please." I squeeze her hand, wanting her to know I'm glad she's alive and well and I'm okay, but right now I need to be alone.

She nods and dresses and she and Dominick are gone in under a minute. I pace around the room, trying to sort it all through.

Never mind processing the fact Anna's still alive; my future is on the line right now.

I told you before that celebrities have been known to fake their deaths. That regular people have been known to do the same. And here I am, faced with the choice to do just that.

I'm to blindly trust the faction who won't reveal themselves to me, other than the tantalizing face of a friend I loved and lost, and the man I recently found a connection with. Can I trust Anna and Dominick? Maybe. Can I trust the faction they represent? Maybe. Can I trust X? Definitely not, but at least his motivations are clear. What he wants is clear. What does the faction want?

They want me to publish the article and take X down. It all seems so simple on the surface when it's stated like a fact. My article will be high profile, especially seeing as how there's scandal around my name, bumping me up into relevance. Even if it's tinged with the video, it will bring attention and the authorities will come sniffing around X. They'll find out exactly how shady his dealings are, substantiating my claims, and arrest and charge him. Justice will be served, reigning supreme, and we'll all live happily ever after and fuck off into the sunset.

Except that's not it. There are more extenuating facts. Like the fact that I'll be exposing myself, transforming myself into the bastard's biggest target. And even if the authorities manage to not fuck it up long enough to arrest him, there's no saying the charges will stick—or that he won't simply get off with a slap on the wrist or a white-collar sentence where he's free to plot his revenge while making some new crooked contacts in his low security resort.

If I don't write the article he wants, he'll likely dispose of me. Hell, after the things I did to him, that's basically a foregone conclusion anyway, and I'm not likely to get off with a nice clean exit. No, he's going to make me suffer, probably to teach others a lesson through me. If I write the one that should be written, exposing the truth, he'll either kill me or The Juliette Society will assist me the same way they helped Anna get away from him.

Either way, Catherine dies. I die. Faked death or genuinely taking my last breath, my life is going to be over forever. No great loss in the grand scheme of things. What's one tiny life compared to the billions who have lived and died before me, and the innumerable ones who will come after?

But priceless is not the same thing as worthless. What's a life worth? If I take the noble route, does that increase the value of myself through some nebulous, objective morality I don't truly believe in? If karma's real, this would be guaranteeing amazing things to come in my future, but I don't put much weight in karma, either.

Is this choice truly mine? Is there a choice at all? It's disturbing how closely it mimics X's perverse love of eugenics, only in this case I'd be giving my life, literally or figuratively, for the untold multitudes of those who would die of this virus—or at the very least, be profoundly affected by it. One life for the good of many others. It seems like a no brainer when you're just crunching numbers.

But is my life a fair trade for the quality of life of strangers and their babies? What about my family, my hopes and dreams, and the potential I have living within me? What is all that worth? Is it worth more than them? No one knows where the ripples on the pond will go, who their efforts will touch and affect. Maybe something I create will inspire someone to create something else, or provide a nexus or inspiration for something that changes the shape of the world.

Or, maybe it will inspire evil. Maybe the biggest gift I can give to the world is not a creation born of my soul and heart, but my disappearance from the fabric of history. My ending may be the best thing I've ever done for the world. But is this plan truly one of global import and consequence? Is it necessary?

Anna and Dominick and whoever the hell else were involved in this scheme certainly seem to think so. One of the most basic instincts of a human being is survival. It goes against some fundamental spark at the base of ourselves to truly give up. I'm a fighter. And throwing my life away because of Mr. X feels so damn wrong I want to scream. It's like admitting defeat. Even if my sacrifice takes him down, he'll think he bested me and there's nothing I can do to contradict that without blowing the whole thing apart.

Because the other law of the jungle is that assholes have friends, and if not friends, allies. Secrets turn to honeycombs, stuck together and intricate until you can't pull one out without the rest being exposed. X is sure to have insurance when it comes to his safety.

The faction likely has a way around this. I hope. Their methods seem inexact, if I'm going by the car crash Dominick orchestrated. And yet, they were successful when it came to Anna and her new life. She's still alive and right beneath X's nose.

They seem to know what they're doing, but they're asking so much. If I declined, would they turn against me?

Would they trade my life for the story? In a heartbeat. But they're trying to save me, give me another existence even as they would gladly snatch my identity away as a fair trade. They're giving me an option—or making it seem like they are.

It all comes back to the question of free will. Is there such a thing? And if not, then in my subconscious, I've already made my decision.

We're all just waiting on me to act upon it.

# TWENTY-SIX

∽oℑℑℑℑ∾

MY DECISION TO WRITE THE article and sacrifice myself, choosing a faked death because, fuck X, is solidified within the next three hours.

After wandering around my villa and unsuccessfully wishing things would go away on their own so I wouldn't be faced with an impossible choice, I dug a little deeper into the materials Anna and Dominick left, and it goes even deeper than I thought.

Part of me was hoping that they'd been lying or embellishing the truth about the things Mr. X had done and was into. They weren't. If anything, they'd downplayed how far he's gone with genetically modifying viruses and releasing them into parts of the world no one really thinks is suspicious when an outbreak occurs.

In more than a few countries—Africa, Cambodia, El Salvador. It doesn't matter that the places he chose to test were small and impoverished and those living in them were likely struggling with day-to-day life. They deserved a chance to live as much as every single person born on this planet. The odds aren't ever on our side, but the way he's so cavalier about the lives of thousands of people sets me on edge. I confirmed it with searches outside of the materials given to me, my due diligence.

For a moment there I sort of regretted doing what I'd done to him at his party.

Not anymore. Now I wish I'd done more, humiliated him more, gone more extreme with people watching him being debased. He cares nothing for anyone but himself. It's hard to regret doing mean things to someone truly evil.

The truth needs to be told. He'd burn the world to kill one person he thought may have slighted him. I'm definitely dead either way, but I can put an end to his insanity.

With a stiff drink to drown out the disgust at the things he's done, I type up an article for my editor. It's the most controversial, damning piece I've ever written. It covers everything from Ebola to the Zika virus and the Rockefeller conspiracy—which isn't the focus and I can't substantiate, but if I allude to it, I know the sensationalism will draw more people to read it. People want to believe that the rich and influential are out to get them.

In this case, with X, they're not wrong at all. Specifically, he's out to get me. And so I'm doing the one thing I can that ensures I go out with a bang.

But submitting this article means I'm finished—as a journalist and as Catherine.

It's bittersweet, but mostly bitter. I'd wanted there to be a legacy of some kind. We all want to leave our mark on the world. We want our time on this rock to have mattered to someone—preferably to as many people as possible.

In my heart, there were so many visions I never got to bring into being. Artistic pieces with impact on the world. Intellectual ones designed to make the viewers think about the world they live in and take away a sliver of truth from it. Even if it's only about themselves, for the best art is a mirror reflecting the best parts—or the ugliest parts of humanity, and makes us want to change into something better.

And now, this is it. This will be the last thing I give, the last creation with my name on it. An article filled with the evil deeds of a worse man. It's stark and powerful and I hope it saves the people I'm sacrificing myself for.

I read it again for errors, tweaking a few sentences here and there for impact and flow, and then type up an email to my editor, attaching the document to it.

Before I can hit send, it's everything I want, and yet the complete opposite as well. I wanted justice for those he's hurt, but what I want and my sense of right and wrong argue with each other as to what is the best outcome.

*This would be justice.*

I don't get to decide who lives and dies. I don't have the right.

*He didn't have the right when he killed those other people.*

I can't let him win. I can't let him continue on killing people—and let him ultimately kill me, whether literally or figuratively. I won't let that bastard win. My hands clench into fists at the idea of making that a reality. I'm dizzy with the hope of not having to give every-thing of myself up, because we are who we are, and I don't want to become someone else when I've just discovered who I am at the core of myself.

I'm wondering why, if this is what needed to happen the whole time, why I am the one who has to do it? I suppose I'm capable of harming someone. I've whipped and been whipped and hurt people and liked it. However, harming someone and taking their life is a completely different thing. And yet, I want him dead. I want someone to get rid of him but hesitate at the thought of being the one to do it.

Ah, but taking someone's life for the right reasons, surely that's the difference? He's killing thousands, maybe millions more will die. This way I could solve the problem and keep my life.

Rattled at the prospect of taking a life, I delete the email. I leave the room, shaking and cold, lips numb with shock, legs stumbling and clumsy as I tear my way down to the house phone to make a call that will change everything, dialing like my fingers aren't mine but stranger's limbs they've sewn onto me and I'm learning to use.

I'm the Mismade Girl.

Like in the stage illusion, also called "The Mismade Girl"— which, strangely enough, was partially devised and performed by Orson Welles—in which a woman climbs into a segmented box and is sawed in four. The boxes are rearranged by the magician, and opened up again to reveal that her body has been reconfigured beyond the laws of physics and biology. The boxes are then put back in order, opened up, and she is revealed to be whole again.

Only I'm not whole yet. After everything I've gone through during the course of my journey in The Juliette Society, and all the ways my world has been turned inside out and upside down, I've been completely taken apart.

Who will I be at the end of this? How will I come out of my experience whole again, remade anew?

# TWENTY-SEVEN

THERE'S ONE THING THAT CAN take any horrible thoughts I'm having and transform them into nothingness.

Sex.

The great equalizer.

Dominick and Anna are hanging out in the foyer, giving me space but sticking around instead of leaving. I'm glad for that. I don't tell them what I've decided to do. They don't ask, and they probably have more than an inkling, but right now I need to forget about that.

"Bedroom. Now," I say, and they follow without words, following my lead as I strip my clothes off on the way, so we all end up naked when we reach the bedroom.

I push Dominick so he is lying on his back on the bed. He's already hard, maybe because he's about to be in a threesome, or maybe because Anna is crawling over the bed towards him, looking over her shoulder as she gives me a show. She straddles his legs and leans forward, licking her hand and rubbing his balls and cock, jerking him off with her wet hand.

I'm content to watch for a moment as Anna moves up and shifts her weight forward, positioning her pussy against the top of his shaft, and slowly slides it back and forth, leisurely, leaving his cock shining with her juices.

I gather her hair in my hands, sweeping it off her shoulders so I can kiss and nuzzle the nape of her neck. She shivers and presses down on Dominick's cock, grinding hard now with little moans and pants. He grits his teeth and groans, looking me in the eyes over her shoulder. I wonder if his cock can feel Anna getting wetter against him because of the way I'm pulling her hair and nibbling her earlobe.

She reaches back, her nimble fingers seeking my clit, and she works it in time with her hips swiveling on Dominick's cock.

"Kiss him," I tell her.

She leans down and places her hand on his chest, the fingers splayed wide as her lips meet his.

But I only want her to do that so my lips can meet the ones between her legs. Bent with her ass in the air kissing Dominick, she's exposed and spread and I lick her from behind. She jumps and gasps into Dominick's mouth, renewing her kiss with a frenzy that tells me she likes the way I'm eating her pussy.

I like the way she tastes, but it's making me ache and feel empty and I need something to fill me up. I wait, giving her more oral attention until her juices drip down my chin like a juicy peach.

"Anna," I say, "I want you to get off and climb on top of Dominick again—but fucking his face this time. Facing me."

Dominick, content to go along with the way I want to play this out, grins as he maneuvers her into the position I want them in.

I swing a leg over his body and guide him to my entrance, and I slam down on his cock, filling my pussy in one hard thrust just as Anna settles over his mouth. He moans up into her, and she likes that, swiveling her hips to take advantage of the vibrations. Her gasp puffs my hair out as her breath reaches my face. We're close enough to kiss.

So we do.

I can't see from here, but the way Anna moves, either she's galloping against Dominick's mouth at a brutal pace, or he's nuzzling her so hard I'm surprised his neck can take it, but our kiss has a rhythm to it.

I'd always wondered what a threesome with Anna would be like.

Except I'd imagined myself with Jack and Anna forming a perfect circle, lying on our sides with our heads buried in one another's crotches. I was sucking Jack's cock, while he ate out Anna's pussy and she was eating mine. We all had a taste of each other. We were all giving and receiving. We were like the snake that eats its own tail. Suddenly I need that more than anything else in the fucking world, and I tell them what I want, and we get up and reposition ourselves and do it. What's sixty-nine plus sixty-nine plus sixty-nine?

It's everything I wanted it to be. Our faces are immersed in one another's laps, sucking, licking, nuzzling for dear life, and it's so good. Anna adds a finger, curling it in that come-hither motion against my G-spot and those thin, perfect fingers of hers are making my hips buck wildly against her smiling mouth, making me suck harder on Dominick's cock—not that he minds.

I taste him more strongly as pre-come oozes from his penis and coats my tongue with the earthy tang, always more concentrated than the come itself. Beginnings are always wilder and more vivid than the endings. Life more earth-shattering than death.

We move, driven by the things we're receiving, which are the input as to what we give. We give the best of what we get, wanting the person we're lavishing with attention to feel as good as we do right in that moment. It's gratitude in a circuit of pleasure, like a battery that is sustained through sensations.

It's like I've always said: you should never have to think about good sex. Your body should just take over automatically when your mind completely relaxes and finally gives up control, letting your body become beautiful and find the release it instinctively craves.

This was exactly what I needed. The little swirls and licks and nibbles Anna's doing feel so good, and I hope Dominick feels the same. I'm tonguing his asshole now while jerking him off with one hand, massaging his balls with the other, and he's not complaining. No, he moans into Anna's pussy, which makes her lick me faster, which makes me lick him faster, and we're all hyping each other up, rewarding each other for a job well done.

Then I feel them repositioning us so we're standing on the floor.

My cunt is on Anna's face and Dominick's behind me, and then all there is, is a cock slamming into me from behind while a tongue laps at my clit from the front. My knees almost buckle as their hands roam all over me, giving me the escape I truly needed, shattering my mind beneath the rhythm of our fucking.

They're making me the star of the show and giving me exactly what I wanted. What I needed.

We're not people anymore, just bodies. Perfect harmony of moans and groans. Perfect rhythm of thrusts and grabs and slaps.

It reduces us to perfect purity of pleasure. They want me to feel the best I've ever felt. I want the same for them. We're aligned with the same goal.

And then I shatter again.

And again.

I'm lying in bed, draped with warm body parts and cool sheets. Anna and Dominick are sleeping, but I'm wide awake, contemplating my life as being this from now on. It could be.

It's a good thought.

But I'm not happy with the way Mr. X is hurting people. How can you enjoy paradise when people next door are in hell? You don't just want a ticket to paradise yourself, you want everyone to get in— and some people are right at the gate but denied and killed. This isn't just about morality and doing the right thing anymore.

I'd always be thinking about the people who would die if I let him live.

But could I really kill someone? I don't think so. I'd rather give someone the chance to turn their life around and make something good come of it, no matter the situation. We all love to root for an underdog, a comeback.

Regardless, I've got to do something and not because a faction wants me to, but because I want to.

Maybe there's a way to get everything I want and more.

They say that the truth shall set you free.

Maybe that's the way to get X to see sense.

# TWENTY-EIGHT

∽⌒⌒⌒⌒⌒

I SHOULDN'T HAVE EXPECTED better from him.

I will maintain, until the day I die, that you cannot buy taste.

Mr. X's place on the compound is set off by itself, on a street with perfect grass and inlaid tiles that probably cost more than most people will make in ten years. It's a gaudy monstrosity of wealth without personality. Pillars, turrets; I'm half surprised there's not a moat. If he could have plated it with gold, I'm sure he would have, creating a monument to his ego.

Then again, he'd likely need his own country for that.

I don't bother knocking when I get to the door. He's expecting me and it's unlocked. I tighten my grasp on the present I've brought him, and encourage her to move a little faster.

It's tough with her on her hands and knees like this.

Inside is worse than outside—another accurate metaphor for the man himself. Marble and crystal and leather thrown together in the most ostentatious combinations possible, as though a stylist from one of those toddler beauty pageants found some contemporary art pieces to design something that they think is classy because of expensive price tag. I doubt he's read any of the books on his shelves.

I pause in front, curiosity rendering me unable to look away, like a traffic accident on the side of the road. I need to know.

I slide a leather-bound volume from the shelf and can tell by the pristine whiteness of the pages, and the stiffness of the spine, that the book has never been read. It's probably never been held except for at this moment in my hand.

Pathetic.

I give myself a shake and put the book back where I found it.

If this half-assed, thrown together plan is going to work, I really need to rein in my bitterness and contempt, lest it show on my face and give the game away. I give the leash a tug and my companion crawls along behind me. As instructed, she doesn't say a word.

Down the hallway I go, looking for an office. I know it will be the one at the very end of the hallway simply because those double doors are the only ones that are closed. The rest are open so I can treat myself to a visual feast of his possessions before getting to him, likely in an office, for the grand reveal.

He's as dramatic as a teenage girl.

Knowing I'm probably on camera, I take my time, wanting to appear relaxed and mildly curious—and for him to get a good look at what I've brought with me. If I seem too dismissive, his feelings may be hurt—not that I give a shit about his feelings, but he's more likely to be closed off and not give me what I want.

At last, I reach his doors and knock, noting that the wood polish is reminiscent of the orange oil from the conference. I enjoy it so much more than the lemon stuff I'm used to back home. This is sweeter, milder, lacking the acrid burn of the lemon version. If I make it out of here alive, I'm going to start using it instead.

I'm going to make a lot of changes.

I reach up and knock twice again.

"Enter."

I push through the doors and struggle not to roll my eyes. His office is a slightly smaller version of Tony Montana's in *Scarface*, right down to the gold ruffled drapes and the red carpet leading to the desk on a raised platform.

There's no giant pile of cocaine that I can see, or machine guns, but the situation is as electric. The air practically crackles with the energy sparking between us.

His smile is tight. "Come in." He beckons from behind the desk, sitting in a large chair—practically a throne, made of some kind of exotic wood and black leather.

The floor beneath the carpet I walk on is some kind of marble tile—Italian, I expect—and I can't tell how large the pieces are. No lines or cracks mar the surface of it. Did they pull slabs this big from a quarry and ship it? Is there one nearby? If it's one piece, the value of it would be astronomical.

I'm impressed at this despite myself, and when I look back at him, I can tell he noticed my interest by the smug smile on his face.

"I'm so glad you could make it," he says, spreading his hands out like he's giving a speech about inclusivity.

"I'm the one who called you to meet," I point out, reminding him that despite his tacky office, I wasn't summoned here.

His eyes flick to my submissive companion—a woman in tight, red latex from head to toe with a full black capped mask dulling all her senses, booties covering her hands and feet—but he doesn't ask. I'm beginning to love that ego of his. I can tell he's curious, but asking about her would put me in the power position.

He focuses on me again. "And here we are. Now, whatever shall we talk about?" He swirls liquor around in a heavy crystal glass.

I manage to smile, a genuine one, but only because I'm picturing the last time I saw him. "I'm not sure about you, but I'd like to talk about the fact that you're a murdering little bastard. A coward who disposes of women."

"My whore has a dirty mouth! Who knew?"

And this is why I've come.

His eyes burn like a zealot who's come to believe his own lies. "You think you're so smart and untouchable because of Penelope? She's no one. She was friends with Inana as well, you know. Ah, yes." He pauses at my gasp. "I know you've suspected. Allow me to clear that up for you. I'm the one who killed Inana, and it wasn't an accident. There wasn't a scene that went too far. I didn't do it for the secret reason some of them believe—that she was going to expose The Juliette Society. I did it because she was a vacuous little whore."

I can't clench my fists or he'll see, but inside my shoes, my toes are cramping, I'm curling them so hard. I'm here for a purpose, but I need him to talk, to tell me everything so I can hear it all for myself and remember why I needed to kill him for everyone's sake.

"I did it because she was Max's and in love with him when she was supposed to be mine."

"You can't own people who don't want to be owned," I exclaim, for Inana wanted to be owned by Max as a kinky submissive, not without agency. "Maybe if you hadn't viewed her as a toy to acquire and respected her—"

"Her what, her art?" He scoffs. "Her little hobby was taking up the time that was better spent with her on her knees in front of me."

"And so you killed her and had them cover it up for you. Did you bribe them to do it? What other secrets are you holding hostage over other people? I can't believe she'd willingly have gone to you if she'd been in love with someone else."

He shrugs. "The only thing she loved more than money was cock."

*Maybe, but it wasn't yours.* "And the rest just went along with it. Max believed it."

He smiles smugly and sips his drink. "He found another toy, soon enough. That's the thing, Cathy. You're all pretty, and entertaining, and utterly replaceable. You think Inana was the only one I've broken and disposed of?" He laughs. "Anna, Lita, Triselle, Donya. I can't even remember the name of the one in Hawaii. She had lips that puffed out like a blowfish. They looked great around my cock. They looked great on her corpse. There was a Russian boy. Ivan... something. You're all so fragile and worthless. No one cares about you enough to do anything."

*Perfect.*

I'd smile if I wasn't getting what I wanted. I'd said the truth would set you free.

You didn't think I meant I was going to tell him the truth about why I'd come—tell him there's a faction trying to kill him and I'm the one they want to be the weapon of his destruction, did you?

The truth that shall set me free is his confession. I'm recording our conversation with my phone, not hoping to get something to blackmail him into incriminating himself for leverage because at this point he's a man whose ego wouldn't stand for being blackmailed. But after, when this is all over, I might need proof that's more substantial than my word against a dead man's...but I wasn't expecting him to give up the goods so spectacularly.

He's giving me everything.

"So, you convinced The Juliette Society members that Inana was going to expose them, and that's why you haven't been put down like the rabid dog you are."

He belly-laughs, which changes to a coughing fit. "Don't flatter me."

"I loved Inana. I loved Anna."

His laughter cuts off as suddenly as it started, and he goes dead-eyed like a fish on a slab waiting to be scaled. "I know. And you'll all be together very soon."

A little of my smugness evaporates at that, but I hold onto my bravado. "Oh? Are you going to kill me next, X?"

He stares at me, breathing for a few moments, enjoying his drink while I wait him out. He speaks first. "You think you're so smart, don't you? You think you can waltz in here with your big eyes and perky tits and get what you want."

"Aw, are you saying you're not attracted to me? Was it something I said, or something I did? Didn't you like our date the other night?"

He squirms in his chair and I'm surprised to realize he actually liked it.

He loved every minute of what I did to him. I bite my lip, confused as to what he's plotting, if not my demise.

"You're not the first who's tried to secretly record me—and I know exactly what you're doing, but it won't work. Go ahead, check your phone, darling. Let there be no secrets between us." His words are sweet but his eyes are deadly.

I don't want to, but I pull my phone out. It's off. I frown and try to turn it on, but nothing. "What did you do?" I ask, uneasy for the first time since I walked up to his door today.

He finishes his drink. "There are perks to knowing people, the way I do. I have friends with their fingers in the pies of all kinds of neat sectors. Technology and communications, for example. I have to hand it to you, you're braver than the others."

He says it to break me, but I bury the agony that flashes through me at his words beneath rage. My stomach tenses and I swallow back bile that scorches my throat. Inana was like a hero, a muse to me, and he killed her like she was nothing. He thought he did the same to Anna. He's done the same to thousands, maybe tens of thousands of other people with his designer virus experiments.

And yet, I'm still breathing. Why am I the anomaly?

Fate? Demons? The will of a tyrant? The boredom of a god?

Is it because he wants to draw out my fear, really savor it down to the last drop before he finally stops playing with me and takes me out of the game entirely? I figured out long ago that his true weakness, ironically, is that he's all about power; a power fetishist, really. But his fetish swings both ways, it seems.

Instead of freaking out, I need to use that to my advantage. Because him disabling my recording hasn't saved him or convinced me to reconsider what I'm about to do.

I slip my jacket off, nonchalantly as though the jig is up and it's all over. "I don't know if I'm braver than the others, but I'm different than them. You're right about that. I came to apologize, tell you I'll write your story, but I also wanted a little guarantee. That's what this little present is for. " His eyes slide up and down my arms and body as I fold the jacket and set it in a chair in the corner, taking my time when I walk back to my seat.

I channel every classic movie vixen when I cross my legs and place my elbows on the armrests, because what he wants is a show. What all men like him want is a show. They don't care about the reality of us—they want the fantasy more than anything, because the fantasy is all about giving them what they want without ever rejecting them. The fantasy never has a headache or a boyfriend she loves more than you.

She's always there for you to project upon. Just like waitresses and sexy cops and every other uniformed stereotype we dream about in the dark while erasing their identities.

I smile. "You liked what I did the other night. I wasn't sure if you'd be able to handle it, X."

"I can handle anything," he snarls. "Anything."

Daddy issues? Abuse? Was it nature or nurture that warped this thing in front of me into the shape of a man? "So I saw," I demure. "You more than proved that to me." I uncross my legs, giving him a flash of panties, and I wish I'd worn none.

It does the trick anyways, and his hand reaches for his glass again before he realizes it's empty. I stand and take the decanter, pouring him a refill so he doesn't feel powerless and threatened. It's a delicate balance; a hair in either direction, and I'm not fucked— I'm dead.

"I wasn't expecting you to like the things I did, X. I was expecting you to be mad, furious at me for doing them. But you aren't. You passed the test and I see in you something I feel in myself. I thought Inana was like me. I didn't know anyone else on the island shared the same proclivities. There's a word for people like us, X. Do you know what it is?"

"Sadomasochists."

Interesting—and along the lines of what I think he is. I incline my head and hand him the glass, letting my fingers touch his. "Free."

His eyes narrow thoughtfully and pulls his hand away, taking a sip. "Go on."

"You and I know there's limits others live by that we eschew. Pleasure or pain. Dominate or submit. It's like cutting off one of your arms. Why live with half an existence because we're taught that half a life is all we should want?" I'm using every bit of the training I've had to control my body and emotions so as not to reveal the depths of my revulsion to this man and convince him that his power is sexy.

I realize now that taping a confession from him is out. Even if I got it, he'd sooner kill me than allow me to blackmail him. He may have let me strap him down, blindfold him, gag him, and let two men with large cocks fuck him in the ass, but to let me have any permanent power over him?

Unthinkable.

As long as it's the bedroom, his ego would allow it. Outside those walls? He'd rather die.

"Here's your gift." I present him with my companion, giving her leash a tug. This is the first time both of his hands have been visible.

He's got a weapon under the table and up until now, he's been debating about whether or not he'll use it, whatever it is. Gun? Knife? Poison in a glass?

"You never offered me a drink," I chastise him.

"This is worth forty thousand a bottle," he replies.

I wink at him. "Then make mine a double. I'm worth it."

And I brace my hands on the arms of his chair, and turn it away from the desk, to separate him from whatever he had hidden. I walk around him in a slow circuit, letting him see my nipples jutting proudly out in front of me. Letting him see my tight ass as I walk for him, swaying my hips as I snap my fingers and point at his feet. "Come, puppy."

She crawls over to us on her little booties that match her latex suit and sits at his feet.

I walk behind him, sliding my fingers through his hair. "Puppy likes to use her feet. Why don't you uncover them for her?"

His fingers fumble to remove the booties and reveal my puppy's pretty pink toes and blood red nails. He guides her toes to his crotch, and she rubs his cock through his pants.

I whisper in his ear. "I wanted to do so much more to you. You know, the worst part was that I had to leave, instead of staying to watch what those men did to you. Did they fuck you hard?"

He nods and his cock peeks up over the top of his pants like the Loch Ness monster rearing its ugly head above the surface of the water. He jerks his pants down and she pinches the skin of his cock between her toes. He gasps as she cradles the shaft between her arches and begins jerking him off with her feet.

I smile, not faking my happiness at hearing that he got fucked hard because of me. "Did it make you sore the next day?"

He nods again and jerks my puppy up to her knees. "Does puppy use her tongue like a good bitch?"

"Why don't we let her use her hands first?" I unbuckle the booties and she flexes her fingers with a slow sensuality, stretching out the show, before she grabs him and starts stroking with frantic tugs at his hairy cock. I shudder, but with my forced moan, he thinks it's out of desire.

We see what we want to see.

I shove her out of the way and spin him around again so I'm standing behind him, leaning down. I reach down and viciously pinch his nipples. He jumps and groans through clenched teeth.

"I want to fuck your asshole," he says.

"I want to fuck yours," I counter. "What a delicious relationship one like this could be," I whisper in his ear, nipping it between my teeth. He nods.

He's in a vulnerable position and I almost hate to admit it, but I'm wet. Not because of him, but because a relationship like this would be hot under different circumstances with someone very different.

What's that say about me?

"Puppy? Stand." She does. I walk around the chair, carefully untangling the leash before handing it back to her.

And in one fast jerk, she pulls the leash tight, choking him with it, bracing her knee against the back of the chair.

His hands fly up to try to get beneath the leather, but he's unable to, and begins making little choking sounds.

"Puppy? Time to show the man how pretty you are." I strip the mask off her and she leans down in his face.

Anna.

Giving her this moment of revenge against the man who took her life seemed only fair. This evens the score.

But a strange sound comes from her and her hands shake.

"Catherine, I can't. I can't!"

She lets go of the leash and I fumble to grab it. "Anna! You wanted this. We need this to happen."

She throws herself on his lap, holding his hands down to the arms of the chair. "Please," she whispers, tears streaming down her face. She lets go of the leash and X claws at his throat, weakly gasping for air. I fumble to grab the leash as it falls. "Anna! You wanted…"

I came to do what needed to be done. To give Anna vengeance. To end this man's horrible existence. Anna was more than game for it. But now that the chips are down, something's holding her back.

Mercy? Regret? What is it that separates her and me? We're so close, so similar, and yet something inside me fights harder to survive.

The part that would never allow anyone to even fake my death slides forth from the shadows inside me, grinning with a knife between its teeth.

I can do this. I can do what Anna can't. "Maybe we're too much alike, X. It could never have lasted anyways." I kiss his forehead and quickly tighten the leash with another twist, looping it back around his neck, and pulling hard, tucking my hands safely behind the back of the chair where he can't reach them.

Surprise and betrayal flash in his eyes but I'm thinking back to Bob, thinking back to times this was sexy, Inana's words flashing through her mind about shattering our own limits.

And then I'm choking X, but all I can see, all I can remember, are other times I've choked and been choked.

DeVille reaching for my wrists, not so he can stop me from striking him again, but to pull them down. Towards his neck.

*He says, "Let's switch. Choke me."*

*His hands are on mine. My hands are on his neck.*

*He says, "Harder."*

*And I squeeze.*

*"Harder."*

*My hard is evidently not hard enough.*

*He says it again and he's shouting it now, over and over and over. Like a sports coach trying to make his athletes burn. And I'm incensed.*

I squeeze as hard as he wanted and now, X's hands flap uselessly up at me as the petechial hemorrhages burst into his eyes, scarring the whites with red. His expensively constructed heavy chair is the perfect shield for me. I'm safe behind his back and he's looking up at me with an expression that's tinged with awe.

What is it that he's seeing, I wonder. I bend a little closer to try and see myself in the reflection of his eyes, to see what I look like right now while killing him.

But my mind flashes with memories of every time I've choked myself, blocking my vision with a haze of nostalgia.

I'm remembering cocks hitting the back of my throat when an enthusiastic recipient of a blowjob thrust a bit too far or too suddenly for me to avoid it.

I'm thinking about fantasies where men seduced me and wrapped silk scarves around my neck and played with my breath like it was their God-given right to take it away.

I'm remembering the interest I've buried and just now been reminded of, in auto-erotic asphyxiation but I was never brave enough to delve deeper into it, for fear of going too far and not waking up after I came and being found in an embarrassing position by a loved one or a stranger.

I'm thinking about choking on words I never got to say to people I love and how I'll never swallow them back again, because any day could be our last and I won't squander an "I love you," from this day forward.

All these and more superimpose themselves over the reality of what's happening right now in this room. I even think of the times I metaphorically choked, and never went for the things I should have because I was scared to want more than I thought I deserved, and that above all else makes me angry with myself. I could have wasted my life and been killed like I was nothing tonight.

But now it won't, because I refuse to be a victim to this choke.

This whole thing has been a metaphor for my life, my desires, my wishes and needs. This is horrible and important and something I never thought myself capable of.

This is necessary.

This is me taking back control. This is me saying to the universe that I will not be snuffed out; that I will fight and struggle and take whatever it gives and give back even more of the same so it had better not try to fuck with me or the people I love ever again.

Some people walk up to the void and step back.

This is me going one step further.

I am Karma, bringing balance to the life and the universe, so watch your back.

I am Kali. Power, change, destruction, liberation. So watch your front as well.

Catherine is not going to die today. I do not live in the shadows like a beaten down stray mutt. I've still got things to say and dreams to breathe life into.

I am breathing heavily and smiling as the tension leaves X's body and he slumps into a heap of meat.

I hold on for what feels like another five minutes, but is likely way shorter, tightening the makeshift noose to ensure that his ghost, if there is one lingering about, knows there's no way he's coming back from this.

There's no way that I'm coming back from this.

I've moved from innocence to experience, from an ingénue to a genius of sex. And every experience has made me empowered by my sexuality, rather than conflicted by it, and I think that is a story worth telling—a positive thing in a culture that does so little to educate young women as they move into adulthood about their bodies and desires; and, at the same time, denies and marginalizes the sexuality of adult women. There's power in sex. Power in getting to know every inch of yourself inside and out and exploiting the things you can do for pleasure...and as weapons.

Wield the things you learn about yourself and no one can ever harm you with them.

X can never harm anyone with his actions or words or power or wealth ever again. He's nothing. The world he thought he ruled for so long is the one that took me in and nurtured the parts deep within me that made it capable to find the strength within to do what must be done.

Right, wrong, it is what it is.

And the part of me roaring with righteousness inside my chest is inordinately pleased that I was the one to reduce his awful existence to this.

If it's any consolation, I'm pretty sure this is exactly the way he'd have wanted to go out. Naked with an erection, strangled with a leash by a woman half his age.

When I'm certain Mr. X is dead, when my heart slows back down to a bearable pace, I sit at X's desk and pick up his phone. Anna shakes from head to toe, but the relief and gratitude in her eyes pleases me.

I punch in the number I was given, wondering if he'll even be a little bit surprised to hear from me.

"Bob DeVille, here."

I take a deep, cleansing breath. "Hello, Bob."

"Catherine?"

"I need your help."

# TWENTY-NINE

∽൘൘൘∾

NOW THAT THE ADRENALINE'S WORN off a bit, Anna and I pant and lean heavily against the door of my place, keeping it locked behind us as Bob instructed me on the phone. I'm not sure if I liked leaving X's body—part of me wants whomever Bob sends to clean up the situation to know it was me who did it.

Would Bob take credit for that? Credit, blame… There's a knock at the door.

Of course there is.

Anna jumps and whimpers.

"No matter what, it will be okay," I whisper, truly believing it.

Funny, she's the one cowering with fear and shame, since I'm the one who should have the guilty conscience. Bob said to lay low when we got out of there. Since I no longer believe in coincidence, I motion for Anna to hide. I wait until she's safely hidden away before moving to the door, though I do pause to grab a heavy bookend to use as a weapon if need be. Yeah, even after what I just did, I'd do it again to protect her, to protect me from retaliation.

Standing on my tiptoes, I peek through the peephole.

There's a man with a tattooed face standing there on my doorstep.

That fucking pink doughnut will haunt me to the end of my days.

I grin and jerk open the door, closing it behind me to give Anna two safely closed doors between herself and the outside world. "Bundy?"

His eyes widen with pleasure and surprise, and a little chagrin at the details surrounding this meeting—his wardrobe choice is something else—and he gives me an outlandishly formal bow and presents me with a thick, vellum envelope.

I grin at how ridiculous Bundy Tremayne looks in a bowtie and brown suit vest paired with satin shorts with knee socks. His legs are so white and scrawny his knees stick out. I tilt my head. "Did you lose a bet?"

"Something like that."

"Did it involve someone here or did you do something before you got to the compound?"

He scratches his face and smirks. The laugh lines are a little deeper in his face, so his life mustn't have been all terrible in the years it's been since we last saw each other. He crosses his arms. "I'm not supposed to say anything in case it influences you one way or the other. There may or may not have been an incident with a salami and a Ukrainian woman, but you won't get the details from me. You're supposed to open the envelope."

Seeing him gives me a lighthearted moment of "the gang's all here," though we're not—and things definitely aren't completely lighthearted at the moment. But it makes me wonder who else is in the compound, sipping a fancy drink by a pool, or who else was at some of those parties I went to.

Was Bundy at the party Penelope threw for me?

Was Kubrick wearing a stylized mask at the surrealist party? Maybe he was fucking someone. Maybe he was fucking someone while wearing a gorilla mask. Hell, maybe he was being fucked by someone wearing a gorilla mask. Either scenario is as likely as the other.

I smile and open the envelope, wanting to ask Bundy about any mutual friends, but deciding to wait in case I spoil the surprise.

It's an invitation to someone's place, written in a careful, elaborate font. I always meant to learn calligraphy but never found the time…or had the patience for it. There are a lot of hobbies I've been interested in but never gotten to. There have been even more that were idle interests; something I thought might be cool to try when I saw, but promptly forgot about.

Fire-twirling. Napkin-folding. Making sculptures out of magnetic sand. Are these things lost to me now if I'm to take some form of punishment for killing X, even though it was the right thing to do?

There's only one way to find out for certain.

Curious, and knowing the timing has meaning to it, I decide to go with Bundy. He turns and I follow him, noticing the tail attached to the seat of his shorts. I'm about to give it a friendly tug when I realize it's actually peeking through the seam of the ass of the shorts.

It's a butt plug with a luxurious faux fur tail attached that swings and swishes when he walks.

Bundy must have really done something naughty to be being punished this way on top of being treated like a lapdog. For someone who prefers to be on top, this punishment seems to be against his nature. He's going along with it rather well, a spring in his step and everything.

I wonder if he knows Anna is alive, but I don't ask, for asking about her reveals she's here, and if he doesn't know that, it's for a reason.

Besides, it's not my secret to tell.

But I can't see him knowing she's here—and knowing what we've just done—and not mentioning it. Perhaps his orders are stricter than I thought, for all the frivolity.

Bundy leads me in silence, to the plainest villa on the street, and I know that whoever lives here is important, because like the grail in Indiana Jones, whoever is in charge here doesn't care to show off their money. They aren't trying to impress anyone with possessions or flashiness. The simplicity is deliberate. Us all being here is the best show of influence and power they need.

Bundy opens the door and leads me inside the dark, cool hallway to a room like a confessional booth at a church, and closes it behind me.

Shut in the darkness, I take a seat on the velour cushioned bench and wait. I'm surprisingly calm, but maybe it's because my body and brain have finally hit saturation point and can't react to anymore shocks at this point.

A moment later, there's a little bump as their door opens then closes on their side of the ornately carved wooden screen that separates us. A bit of light shone through when their door opened, showing me the details of the partition. It's so smooth and fine I could probably push my fingers through it like tissue paper, but I don't for obvious reasons.

Then it too swings open, revealing the smiling face of...Bob DeVille. "Catherine."

"Bob, I—"

"Come with me, don't be nervous, Penny is here," he interrupts and opens the partition between us, leading me through the door into a larger room with one large chair and twelve slightly smaller surrounding it, which form a circle. All except two chairs are empty. "Mine, and yours," he says, taking his seat.

I take mine as well, avoiding eye contact with anyone except Penny and Bob. Their intense scrutiny makes me feel like a bug in a jar which annoys me, and I throw my shoulders back and boldly look them in the eyes. I'm not a scared little girl they can intimidate. Whatever they've got planned, I can more than handle it.

The woman in the most ornate chair inclines her head to me. "Welcome, Catherine." Her voice is warm and rich like melted butter. "It's a pleasure to finally meet you." She's in her late forties with a heart-shaped face, silky chocolate skin, and wide brown eyes that remind me of Inana's. Her hair is pulled back tight in a perfect chignon, and her clothing reeks of class and wealth without making show of the fact that she is the leader.

I was relaxed, sure. But maybe my pulse kicks up a little that she's not some alpha asshole businessman in a suit. Then again, it's *The Juliette Society*—so what else could I expect other than a woman to be the one in charge? The hint's been there in the name all along.

I lean closer. "Thank you," I reply. I smile. "I liked your delivery boy."

She chuckles. "Ah yes. Bundy and you have a history. I was hoping it would amuse you."

I grimace. "You didn't make him wear that tail just for me, right?"

"No. That was to atone for other actions of his own making. He's nearly redeemed himself and can go back to his shenanigans soon. I'd never tell him, but he does keep things interesting around here."

That makes me feel slightly better for my...well, I wouldn't call him my friend, but I'd hate to know he's forced to serve some asshole like X for the rest of his life. He deserves to cut loose in a place like this where the girls don't need drugs to fuck, unless it's that kind of party. Maybe he found a large woman with seventies pubes like he dreamed of.

But I've come here not to talk about my old acquaintance or for a girly chat. "This place is yours?" I ask, meaning so much more than the house we're sitting in.

"In a manner of speaking. If I told you it's mine now but not forever, that would be accurate."

"Have you known about me all along?" Somehow, speaking in front of the others feels natural instead of like we have an audience.

"Not much escapes my notice when it comes to the world we've created."

Somehow her confession doesn't creep me out. It's sort of like having a guardian angel watching over me, even if she's not always done a great job of protecting me from harm. Speaking of X...

"You brought me here to discuss something in particular."

When she speaks next, I can hear the smile on her lips in her words. "I do so love your directness, Catherine. It's been brought to my attention that we have a mutual…issue."

"If you're talking about a certain pretentious asshole with a one letter name, then I took care of it." My impatience overtakes me. "X killed people. He killed some of our members. He tried to kill me by destroying my career and reputation."

"Not all who are dead stay dead."

My blood runs cold. Did I not kill him? Did I let go too soon and his heart stuttered back to life after Anna and I left? Impossible. "I know he's dead."

"I was speaking of you, not him."

I unclench my fists and uncross my legs. "What are you talking about?"

"You almost went there a couple times, but something always held you back from that final push. The stakes never changed—things were always life or death."

They knew all along I was in danger, but didn't think to step in? "Surely you have people who could have…neutralized the threat."

Bob laughs softly and tells me that this wasn't about just taking him out. "It was a final initiation—whether or not you were ready to take your rightful place of power."

I frown. "My rightful place?"

The woman nods. "We have watched you for a long time, evaluating your choices. We believe you have proven yourself to be a valuable asset."

"What about Anna?"

She smiles. "Your friend is a favorite to many of us, but even you must realize there's a fundamental difference between you and her."

Back at X's, I'd literally handed revenge to Anna on a platter and she'd been unable to take what was hers. "She knew everything I did about X and was still unable to do what I did."

"Precisely." The woman gestures to those around us. "Not everyone is suited to this lifestyle. Even fewer are able to do the things we in this room do to protect The Juliette Society and ensure its survival. But you, Catherine, have earned your place here—if you want it."

There's a poetic justice in cutting the head from a hydra and seeing your own face spring forth. By killing X, I've won the opportunity to become the beast, merge with it, grow stronger with it.

I look at Bob, and his smile is enigmatic. Penny nods like she knew all along I belong here. Each person in this room has power. Each person in this room knows exactly who they are.

No fears, no regrets, no excuses. They'll do whatever it takes to get what they want and protect the people they love. To be true to themselves, even though it's not always the easy path.

And they think I'm one of them.

I lean back in my chair, sliding my hands over the arm rests with a smile, because you know what?

They're right.

# EPILOGUE

SOMETIMES ACTIONS HAVE CONSEQUENCES you'd never dreamed possible. Even if you get away with something, it can feel like there's another shoe waiting to drop. It's all about the anticipation in that case, even if it's not, because you're looking forward to whatever may come next.

And sometimes, nothing happens except for the changes inside you that are invisible to the rest of the world. You carry on with your days, weeks, months, years. You live your life the way you want to live it.

No fear, no regrets. Until one day you look back and decide which decisions you made were the right ones. Which things you'd have done differently to get you to the optimal place a little faster.

And you want to share the hard-won lessons you learned with someone worthy of the knowledge.

And that, my dear, is the reason you're here right now.

But before we go any further, let's get this out of the way: I want you to do three things for me. No, not stop, drop, and roll—although in a sense, your world is about to catch on fire.

If you want it to.

So, one: Do not be offended by anything you read beyond this point.

Two: Leave your inhibitions at the door.

Three, and most importantly, so pay attention: Everything you see and hear from now on must remain between us.

Okay. Now let's get down to the nitty-gritty.

When I told you that a secret club exists whose members are drawn only from the most powerful people in society: the bankers, the super-rich, media moguls, CEOs, lawyers, law enforcement, arms dealers, decorated military personnel, politicians, government officials, and even distinguished clergy from the Catholic Church—did you believe me?

Or did you think I was speaking hypothetically?

I wasn't talking about the Illuminati. Or the Bilderberg Group, or Bohemian Grove, or any of those corny plot devices used to advance the commercial agendas of disingenuous conspiracy nut jobs.

No. This club is a lot more innocent—on the face of it.

But not underneath where I've peeled back the lies and showed you the truth.

This club meets irregularly, at a secret location. Sometimes remote, and sometimes hidden in plain sight. But never the same place twice. Usually not even in the same time zone.

We call it The Juliette Society.

Maybe now you get my drift. Maybe now you understand why this secret society, The Juliette Society, might not be as entirely innocent as it seems.

And when I told you that I'd managed to penetrate—pardon my French—the inner circle of this club, did you believe me? How about now, after all I've shared with you? Does it make you hungry for more? What is experience worth to you? And what does it cost?

And they're not the same thing at all. One is concerned with meaning, the other with sacrifice.

We're so used to paying a price—for our weekly shopping, our health, our mistakes, our indiscretions, and other crimes, affronts, and misdemeanors—and never questioning how much, or who decides what that is and why. And, as a culture, we seem obsessed with what's been lost—whether it's innocence, privacy, privilege, security, or respect—rarely with what's been gained.

No one but no one can tell me what my experience is worth. No one but me. It's something only I can know and understand and feel. It's something only I can weigh up, measure and quantify. Something I can choose to pass on to others or keep for myself. And that's my choice, and my choice alone. It's my freedom to decide. My responsibility to uphold.

Let's not mince words here. We're talking about sex. About fucking. And everyone does it, whether in public or in private. More or less. Straight or kinky. Solo or in pairs or groups. With the opposite sex or their own. And, in practice, usually several or all of the above options in combination. Our sexuality is as at least as complex as our personality; maybe more so, because it involves our bodies, not just our minds.

This isn't about science, it's about being. And that's why I don't particularly trust the conclusions of people like Doctor Kinsey and Doctor Freud, especially when it comes to women. Because how do you quantify or categorize desire? How you can make value judgments on what's good or bad for people, for individuals, based on how they feel? Based on how they fuck?

We're all freaks. In secret. Under the skin. In the sack. Behind closed doors. When no one's looking. But when someone is looking, or when someone knows, that's when there's a price to pay. A price that's put on us, like a pound of flesh. And that price, it might be called many things, when it's really just one thing.

Shame.

But by now you should know that shame is a construct designed to keep us from claiming our power. Some of us are able to throw off the shackles of that word, that concept they've tried to hold us down with.

I have it.

Inana had it.

Anna has it.

We could argue back and forth forever about nature or nurture, but this talent, it's not something I was born with. At least not that I'm aware of. No, this is something I realized. But it has been with me for a long time, hard-coded, buried like a switch in a sleeper agent, and only recently turned on.

I see that same talent in you.

Now, the time has come to decide. This story has become about what you want. How far you'll go.

Do you remember what the three stages of initiation are? Let me remind you.

Disorientation of the senses. Intoxication of the body. Orgiastic sex.

Everyone's kinks are different. Taking the ultimate risk for some doesn't involve hands around your throat, letting them choke you within an inch of your life. Sometimes the ultimate risk is reaching out to someone.

The way I've done with you.

You're here now, reading these words because you want to know what it tastes like to savor a life like this. But you'll need to ask yourself, "What is experience worth? And what does it cost?"

This is what my experience is worth: I understand things now about sex and power and how they connect and interact that some people never get to discover during the course of their entire lives. And I didn't know what the future held when I killed Mr. X, but I did always know one thing that was not in the future I saw for myself: Being a whistleblower.

My instinct for survival was and is a lot stronger than my desire to save the world. So I could play the hero if I wanted to, but do I want to be known as that person for the rest of my life? Do I want to live with the consequences? What would my life be then? Secrets are best kept, not revealed. This one has stayed with me. But I reserved the right to change my mind at any time.

What would you have done in my position?

Do you want to find out?

See, this is how these things work. You need to know that. No one has any incentive to go public. It's not in anybody's vested interest.

That's the true nature of power. The occult nature of power. It's hidden. And it remains hidden. So The Juliette Society, it just carries on. Girls like Anna will continue to disappear. Or turn up on islands in other countries.

And evil bastards like X will be put down like the dogs they are. Because he's dangerous and doesn't know enough about the bigger picture to realize that he is replaceable. Ultimately, he's one link in the chain that can easily be replaced. It's always been that way and it will always be that way. Mutually assured destruction benefits nobody.

What about me?

What am I getting out of all this? What's the price I'll have to pay and how could I have known? Before the fact, not after; because sex is not a supermarket aisle where you can browse all the different options and know the cost before you make your choice. So let's assume I was fully conscious and aware of everything that I was doing and why. It's far more interesting that way, isn't it? Because there are no excuses. There's no one to blame.

I'm not just talking about the things I did, but about the things I fantasized and dreamed about. The places my subconscious led me. Because it all comes from the same place at its core.

Why would I topple the bricks someone built on my own foundation? When a tree is sick you cut out the diseased boughs, you don't hack down the whole thing and burn it to ashes. But from time to time, you need to plant seeds so new things can grow. Trees are good, forests are better. There's safety in numbers. There's experience in numbers.

Knowledge is power. Sex is the great equalizer.

And I sent you this book you're reading right now for a reason. Because I see in you the same things they saw in me.

So, what do you say? Do you have what it takes to join me on the next step? Me? I'll be with you in spirit, for these events happened to me long ago. They're fresh for you, ancient history to me. I've moved on to other things.

But The Juliette Society? My journey's ending but yours is just beginning...

If you're ready for it.

# ACKNOWLEDGEMENTS

THANK YOU TO EVERYONE who had faith in this trilogy and saw it through, and the fans that have maintained passion for following Catherine's journey. This was never intended to be a traditional romance novel, so the support of everyone who understood that *The Juliette Society* was an homage to classic erotica, I thank you for letting me take this chance. To Marc Gerald, Peter McGuigan, and Kirsten Nehaus for the constant faith and input. Cobra Verde. Tamara. To my mentor Anthony D'Juan for never letting me settle for less, or make excuses. To my family and friends for always believing in me. Lastly, to the teams at Little Brown, Cleis Press, Grijalbo, Livre De Poche, Audrey, Heyne, and Markus Naegele, for the love of literature.

# ABOUT THE AUTHOR

**SASHA GREY** first made her name as one of the most notorious adult film stars in recent history; but with a no regrets attitude, she moved on from her former career in 2009 at age 21. She published NEÜ SEX a book of photographs, and has appeared in both traditional films and television, most notably HBO's Entourage. In 2013, she published her first novel, the internationally successful *The Juliette Society*, in 25 countries. *The Mismade Girl* is her third novel. She regularly tours internationally, as an artist, author, and deejay.